MERAKI

NAOMI KELLY

Also by Naomi Kelly:

Trial by Obsidian

Cover Design: Juan Padron

Map Design & Closing Image: Naomi Kelly

To my eternally youthful mother,
Undoubtedly, you'll look for yourself in this book, but
I promise you that this is the only page on which you
feature. You compare in no way to the mother of this
story. You're more joyous, selfless and loving than she
could ever even aspire to be.
But most importantly, you can't bloody swim!

ONE

Have you ever been so tired that even the effort of falling asleep felt like too much work? Well, I have numerous times, and once again this is where I find myself now.

Technically, I find myself drifting about twenty-two miles south of my bed where I should be asleep, but I cannot go back.

Not yet.

Maybe not ever. Maybe that's why I am so damn exhausted. Everyone assumes sea creatures have terrible memories because of lower intelligence, but after three weeks of being underwater, I barely remember my name. At least common fish have the intellect to turn off half their brains to get some rest, but me? No such luck.

I did try to sleep at some stage last week, but yet again, the nightmares sought me out. No matter where I go, they follow.

Instead, I drift and think.... I float and fret.

I begin to hum to myself just to hear another sound, but I cut my tune short. The last thing I need is a pod of whales accidentally summoned to my side. I'm beginning to worry I've conceived every thought possible when I feel a disturbance in the water.

A ripple against my core. It's too small to be a typhoon, yet too large to be the lurking shark who had its beady eye on me for days now.

Straining my eyes to peer through the murky waters, I spot a heavy net drifting downward. It unravels silently and opens its mouth wide like a hungry beast.

There should be no fishermen here, especially at this time of year. Trawling in these waters is always dangerous, but only a desperate fool would venture this far North in winter. Although by the large gaps in their netting that most fish would easily swim through, this fisherman was indeed a fool. Unless he was hunting for a were-dolphin; one of those beasts would keep a family fed for the entire winter.

Weeks of boredom and an inbuilt hunger for curiosity compelled me to swim closer. They did not even have an icebreaker attached to their hull!

Perhaps it would be kinder for me to take them hostage and present them as an offering to the Queen. It could be a win-win situation. I would prevent his slow painful end as he inevitably froze to death, and I might not be immediately turned away from the Queendom gates if I bring her a plaything.

I glide to the left to get a better look at the lone boat blocking the weak winter sun as it looms closer. Then I see it, that crest on the side. This is a royal vessel.

The gills lining my side flare in disbelief, sending a stream of bubbles to the surface. Without hesitating I pump my tail, propelling myself under the keel and out the other side. The boat rotates faster than I thought possible for such a long vessel.

The groan of the wood is muffled but audible underwater as the boat is pushed to its limit to keep up with me. To track me.

Living by dark waters means one must forego paranoia from a young age, otherwise shear insanity would break you.

Every sound, every flash of scales would feel like a threat. One must learn to silence the fear in order to live. Yet as I see the large net aim directly for me, I loathe myself for shunning the fear. I should have been afraid. I should have swum away.

With the net closing in to my left and the jagged rocks of the coastline to my right, the open pool before me is my last resort.

I prepare to lurch forward but pause. I taste the subtle change in salinity. I feel the temperature ever so slightly increase against my skin and notice the smoother, smaller pebbles on the seafloor that's rising quickly to meet me. They're trying to corral me into the shallow cove.

I glance down at my tail. It has offered me speed and protection the past few weeks but now it threatens to kill me. If I am beached, I will not be able to adapt back to land-life fast enough to run away. The weight of the tail suffocates my legs.

Instead, I twist onto my back, looking upwards to see the silhouette of a man leaning over the side of the boat. His dark shadow wobbles in the watery mirror, and for one wasted moment, I wonder who is seeing the greater monster- him or me?

The knotted cords of the net begin to press into my skin as the ropes retract. No longer having an escape route, I opt for a different method.

I contort my body within the ever-constricting space, placing my head against the bottom of the net. I force my outstretched arms through the gaps and wait. My body coils with withheld power.

The figure I saw is not alone. Dozens of hands now clamber at the slack, hauling the loose netting overboard. They work in tandem.

Heave. Stop.

Heave. Stop.

I let them *heave* one more time before using their momentary pause to execute my plan.

Unfurling my body, I thrust my tail towards the surface. If they do not know what they have caught, they certainly do now.

I pump my arms rapidly, cutting through the water before me yet I get nowhere. I ignore the muffled shouts from above and direct all my focus into getting as far below the waves as I can.

Between my frantic flapping and the crowd of captors leaning over the edge, the boat threatens to topple. Capsizing the vessel was not my intention but it's an option I'll take. Let them sink to their watery graves for ever trying to capture me.

The cords embed into my skin as I fight and fail to win back any slack. A crisscross of cord slices into my cheek. The cut deepens the harder I thrash. A trickle of blood and ichor drifts from my face and floats before my wide eyes.

My neck feels like it is close to snapping from the constant force of my downwards pushing. Yet I am going nowhere.

Exhaustion begins to seep in. Bubbles and blood escape, but I do not.

Without notice, the shouting voices cease. The boats rocking settles to an unsettling lull. As the eerie calm descends, my eyes dart to the surface to see the peering audience move away.

All but one.

The same shadowed figure as before remains to stare overboard, watching my every move. His blurry image is abruptly distorted by his fist punching through the icy water.

Grabbing my tail, he tugs hard. I soar through the water as he drags me towards him. Once I'm close enough, he thrusts his open palm into my inky dark hair. With his firm grip on my skull and a fistful of my hair, he easily navigates me.

Once I'm ripped into the air above, arms grabble at me from every direction. Hurrying hands haul me over the wooden ledge, and then dump the net and its contents on the deck.

"I guess I owe you for that bet about not needing an icebreaker then, my Majesty." A man's voice laughs awkwardly without humour as he moves closer. He begins to untangle the ropes and net, but my thrashing body makes it no easy task.

I instinctively claw at my throat. I'm fooled to feel as if I'm drowning in air. He drops the net and restrains my wrists instead.

The bright winter sunlight holds no heat, yet it burns my eyes. I blink away tears and hope they know I weep from the light and not from fear.

They being the crew circling me, staring with whale eyes as if they had never seen a syren before. I'm guessing they haven't.

My eyes scan through all the faces quickly, but trip and stumble over the bastard who keeps a strong grip on my tail. He's paler than the average sunbeaten sailor, and he wears a long, draping dark cloak. The royal emblem of the pointed crescent moon and a lone star is sewn above his heart.

I know not who this pain in the ass princeling is, but I'm sure he is not King Lachlan. With his taut jaw and knitted fair eyebrows, he does not look as animated as the rest. He simply looks...annoyed.

"She doesn't have wings, and why is she not singing, Fletcher?" His growl carries upwards from my tail.

Wings? Syren's haven't had wings for decades and he's acting like he's somehow disappointed! Oh, how badly I want to tail slap him in his gormless face.

"Her *not* singing is what we want right now, my Majesty." The Fletcher man states drily.

He crosses my arms over my torso, attempting to pin my flailing body against the deck, "Besides her kind cannot sing whilst they're transitioning."

My gills slap open and closed as real air begins to fight its way through my flaring nostrils and panting mouth. The sea breeze feels heavy and abrasive, as if there are chunks of salt in the wind, whipping against my pale periwinkle, damp skin.

Skin which I'm pretty sure is now on fire. I cannot bear to open my eyes in the harsh light to check, but my arms blotch and burn as blood vessels lacking oxygen rush to the surface. If I were to look, I'd expect to see my body charred, the wooden deck beneath me steaming as my skin blisters from the internal heat.

"How long will the transition take?"

Seven minutes, I think to myself, but I have no idea how much time has passed. This is what forever feels like. Everything and nothing all at once.

Someone places the back of their hand against my forehead. I hope my skin scorches their knuckles.

"I'm not sure, your Majesty. I've only read of it, yet I fear she is transitioning too quickly. Maybe if we place her in the water it would ease the adaptation?"

Fletcher's voice sounds further away as my heartbeat races through my eardrums, pounding like a herd of centaurs.

I try to rein in my racing mind which is pulsing from the mounting pressure. Even with my eyes closed, spots dance across the back of my eyelids. My jaw pulsates from the growing headache, scrapping my teeth together to form the loudest sound in my skull has ever housed.

"Are you honestly suggesting I put her back in the sea?" The princeling's hostile tone is matched with a tightening grip which threatens to snap my ankles.

I pray to Poseidon, to Zeus, to Oceanus, to whatever god will hear my plea. Either release me from my suffering or give me the strength to kill them.

My gills flap one last time and then close for good. I do not know which outcome the gods shall fulfil.

"No, not all the way into the sea, but-"

The gods choose life.

I lurch at the hips and sit upright. I throw my head back and draw a deep, deep breath. The air tastes euphorically good as it floods my lungs.

Sweet, invisible life force.

I instantly turn the simple air into my weapon. I begin to sing, but little more than a grunt escapes as I'm blown backwards.

"Now!" The princeling roars, as he knocks me onto the deck.

He pins me using his body weight. His large, hot hand slaps over my mouth. I bite deeply into the fleshy part of his palm until a knuckle is wedged between my incisors. He yelps a vile curse, yet he doesn't surrender.

8

Barking orders over his shoulder, the rest of the sailors' obediently scurry away from us. They opt to huddle behind the helm.

Ha! As if those mere few feet would offer them any protection from me.

Fletcher edges forward to hand his Majesty something before backing away in haste to join the others.

The princeling struggles to hold the object in one hand and keep my mouth covered at the same time.

"Do not resist," he says sternly, "I do not wish to accidentally knock half your teeth out."

He fumbles with an iron crafted device single-handedly. It isn't until he unfolds its appendages, I understand what is going on.

It's a syren bridle.

The device is an ancient idea, but this one has a modern twist; it's designed to resemble an octopus. How fitting!

The body of the metal octopus is thin and curved like a spoon. The princeling replaces his chewed knuckle for this. It fills my mouth and immobilises my tongue immediately. I attempt to hum but he lightly slaps my throat with disapproval as if he were swatting a fly.

He sits the stiff tentacles snuggly around my face. Two iron bars go across my cheek on either side, the rest slide under my jaw and press against my larynx.

Great.

Now I cannot even hum. I can barely breathe. The metallic arms meet behind my head where they *click* close under the mop of my wet hair. Once he is satisfied it's secure, he rolls back onto his haunches. He retrieves a damascus steel knife from his under his cloak and leans in close to me.

I stiffen.

He thumbs a lock of hair, folds it in a loop and slices the blade through effortlessly. He holds the fallen tress before my wide eyes. He cut free a barnacle. Without breaking eye contact with me, he flings it back to the sea.

I never in my life thought I would be jealous of a bloody barnacle.

"How much fate do you put in those stories you read, Fletcher?"

"Which part of the tale in particular, your Majesty?" Fletcher asks, remaining where he is but peering over cautiously.

"The *tail* part of the tale." A sardonic smile pulled at the princeling's lips. A few sailors laugh.

I want to drown them all, starting with him.

Everyone's attention turns to Fletcher. He stutters and then sighs before saying, "Well...everything I've studied has been correct thus far."

Seeming content with that answer, he nods to himself before flashing his knife once more. Except now the blade is hovering above my thighs.

Shit.

They know more about my kind than I hoped. Mortals used to believe we had to be returned to the sea every night like our mermaid cousins. They thought we could not function on land, or we would simply shrivel up and perish if our tails ever fully dried. And although this is far from the truth, it helped keep us safe. It helped keep us near water. But if they know the truth, they will bring me inland. Bring me to *their* land.

"Apologies for the crude way we met. I am King Kellan of the Crescent Cove, Meteoroid Spit and Star Spike, collectively known as the Lunar Islands. You will have an opportunity to introduce yourself, eat and drink once we are back on the mainland. Until then you will be kept securely in the hold."

Trusting in Fletcher and his stupid books, he carefully slides the knife into my tail just above my knees. Some of the sailor's gasp, probably expecting to see blood, but there is none.

No wound. No gore.

There is only the glint in King Kellan's golden eyes when he realises the books were right. He traces the blade down the length of my being to reveal my bare legs underneath. As the tail separates from my body, the magic I feed into it fades. It becomes nothing more than a tightly bound skirt made of scales and kelp.

With my feet fully free, he begins cutting above my knees. Although I cannot sing him into oblivion or even protest his actions, I try my best to convey an "*uh-huh*" sound and shake my head frantically. He looks annoyed. Then confused.

I scream inside my head, "*I'm completely naked under the few inches of seaweed you haven't destroyed you fool!*".

Maybe he somehow heard me, or maybe my flitting eyes gave away my problem, but a sense of realisation dawns across his face. My cheeks flush lilac with fury and embarrassment.

"Sailors avert your gaze starboard," the King commands as he stands, no longer looking at me. He shrugs off his cloak and walks towards the helm. Obediently and in unison, half a dozen men turn on their booted heels. They all stand up straight and look across the horizon.

King Kellan taps Fletcher on the shoulder, hands him the knife and his cloak and then takes his place beside his men. Fletcher crosses the few steps and kneels beside me. He fans the cloak over me like a blanket and rips the remnants away without the use of his eyes or blade.

He offers a sympathetic smile, lifts his hand and twists the marriage band on his finger for me to see. I think it's somehow supposed to be comforting that he's a married man. It is not.

I survived the net. I survived the breakneck speed of my forced transition. But this lack of dignity might just kill me.

Gods above, why did you opt to spare my life.

TWO

The "secure hold" I am placed in is little more than a storage area in the cabin of the vessel. Frayed rope, rusted cannonballs, and the old wooden barrel I sit upon make up the contents of the room.

Two of the King's sailors have been guarding me for hours. They remain by the open door, one facing me, the other watching the deck. They rotate their positions like clockwork, without prompt or conversation, and they have not slipped up once. They are better trained than I anticipated and it's infuriating.

The man facing me is staring. Staring at my windswept hair that has snared shells and sand. Staring at my bare legs and hands, the only parts of me visible under this comedically large cloak acting like a poorly fitted dress on me. He stares not from a lack of manners, but sheer curiosity. I doubt he has ever seen a girl with skin that always holds a blue tinge no matter how dry or warm.

Granted, I was not like other girls, but like all women, syren or mortal alike, I knew how to play the damsel card when needed. And it was time to play.

The barrel wobbles as waves crash into the side of the boat. I wait for a large wave to rock the barrel, and then 'fall' to the ground. I lay splayed out in an inelegant fashion, with my back curled to the door and arms flung in the corner. Although my wrists are bound with a segment of the net, my hands are free.

I inch my fingers towards the cannonball in the nest of rope before me.

"Ma'am?" the guard calls as he rushes in. I stay down and even close my eyes for dramatic effect.

As the sailor rolls me over to help me up, I swing my weighted fist towards his face. The cannonball meets his nose and releases an unholy *crunch*.

He falls back, howling and burying his face in his hands. Blood runs down the inside of his sleeve. I stagger to my feet, but the other guard is already blocking the doorway.

He remains in place. Unsure whether to aid his comrade, launch at me or call for backup. I use his hesitation to throw another cannonball in his direction.

I aim for his face, but my arms are too weak, the weight too heavy. It misses and instead lances his shoulder. Not my desired target but it does unsteady him enough to wobble him out of the doorway.

"Your Majesty!" The guard bellows.

I bolt.

All around me, sailors on the deck abandon their tasks. Sails flack as sheets and ropes are dropped. Fletcher frees his hands of the large wooden wheel and uses them to nab me instead, but I rip away from his clawing grasp.

Wind catches the sail and whips the boom across the deck. Two men duck to avoid the soaring pole of wood as it swings back and forth, but I do not take cover. Instead, I turn sideways and skirt the ledge, moving as quickly as I can towards the stern.

I need to get back to the sea.

My weary lungs, barely reacquainted with the notion of breathing, are now labouring hard. The inability to breathe through my mouth because of the damn octopus strapped to my face leaves my flared nostrils to do all the work.

My legs burn and ache as I force them to carry me the last few feet. Even though my frame is painfully bony in parts, I feel entirely too heavy.

Had gravity always weighed so much?

I scramble to climb the waist-high edge of the stern, but with restrained wrists it proves too difficult to pull myself up. I'll have to throw myself overboard from where I am.

I would prefer to dive in, to break the water feetfirst, but I'll take what I can get.

"Wait!" King Kellan roars from behind me, but I do not turn around.

Pacing back a few steps to give myself room to run and vault, I then-

"Look at me," he thunders, his voice louder than the sea and somehow more menacing, "Look. At. Me."

I pause. I hate that I do, but it's instinctual. Obeying stern royalty is a hard habit to break.

Looking over my shoulder to see six sailors stand in a row. The guard I hit in the shoulder and the man with the bleeding nose are on either side of the line-up.

Fletcher is firmly back at the helm. The boom is under control once more. The sails no longer flap frantically. It seems I'm the only wild thing left onboard.

The King is closest to me. He holds his arms out before him in a nonthreatening way, as if I were a spooked animal he was trying to catch.

"Don't you see the White Horses out there?"

He jerks his chin towards the water. I reluctantly glance over the stern.

Poseidon's infamous steeds gallop across the sea. White-tipped waves rise and then break as they collide over the hidden rocks down below. Jagged boulders burst through the water in places and cast ominous shadows in the places where they remain unseen.

For a brief second, I am glad to have the syrens bridle on. It makes my deafening silence less obvious.

He was right.

I was terribly wrong.

This was not a way to earn freedom, it was a way to achieve suicide. My mother said I would not survive outside the clam gates of our world. Perhaps she was right too. Perhaps everyone except me is right in this damn world.

His tensed arm wraps around me in an instant and violently tugs me off the ledge. He hauls me half away across the deck with my feet trailing behind me. He slams me against the mast pole and holds me by the neck.

As if I didn't have *enough* breathing issues.

"Like I said earlier, do not resist or some of those pearly whites of yours might get misplaced," he snaps.

He stays still, staring at me as he waits for a reaction. He remains tight with tension for one too many breaths. Just staring at me, as if he were able to read my thoughts.

I match his gaze and refuse to blink. It is the only control I have left. It seems misleading someone with honey-coloured eyes should be so astringent.

The King drops hold of my throat and shakes my shoulder roughly instead, "I need you to survive, syren."

Releasing a staggered sigh, he looks over his shoulder, "Someone fetch me rope. A lot of it. And attend to Arthur's nose. I can tell from here it's broken."

Men quickly get to work, uttering "*yes, sir,*" and "*of course, your Majesty,*" as they go.

Three reels of rope with varying thickness are placed at the Kings feet for his choosing.

He does not choose. He opts to use them all.

He wraps the ropes around me in both directions, twisting and turning as if I am a Maypole to be decorated with despair.

He ties a complex naval knot I do not recognize and leans in close so only I hear him, "The next time you wish to see the waves up close, I would be more than happy to strap you to the front of the bow. I always thought this ship could use a figurehead."

"Oh, go to Hel!" I snap, although the muffled sound that erupts out the side of lips sounds like gibberish. I try my best to look away from him.

Somehow understand my fiery retort, he grins saying, "My place in Hel is already secure, I'm simply maintaining my reputation."

Even though I'm securely held and have few notions of trying to escape again, tensions remain high onboard for the next hour or so. The men give their moody King a wide berth, opting to watch the seas or me instead.

Fletcher, who I've gathered from overhearing the men, is "*Master of the Sails.*" The highest title a crew member can be given. The reasoning for his title and the tension makes more sense when I realise where we are.

The Meteoroid Spit.

A dense archipelago connecting the most northern tip of the Crescent Cove to the western coastline of the Star Spike in a series of hopscotch islands. I assumed few people inhabited the islands, but I could not have been more wrong.

As we slowly sail our way through the chunks of land, I notice rope bridges spanning the distances between some of the islands in closer proximity.

Sweat glistens across Fletcher's forehead as he nimbly navigates the tightest part of the route. Two sea stacks act like guardsmen, standing tall at the mouth of the Lunar Lands bay.

Children hop from one land mass to the next, sprinting across bridges and jumping over gaps. My heart pounds in my throat.

They're going to fall. I cannot bear to watch them plummet to their deaths.

They continue to run, dashing across the rope bridge which attaches to the sea stacks. The rope shakes dramatically. It looks like it's about the snap, yet more children pour out from nooks and join in the horrible fun. We're so close to the stacks that their faces are visible now.

A young boy scrambles to the top and yanks the awaiting chain. Bronze and gold coloured bunting embroidered with the royal emblem, unfurl and drapes from one sea stack to the other.

Fletcher releases a sigh and rolls his shoulders as we pass through the pillars, "Welcome home, your Majesty."

The King claps his back firmly. He makes a ring shape with his index finger and thumb before placing in his mouth and releasing a loud whistle.

"Good work, Ludwig!" The King shouts to the victorious child, who squeals in delight, "You'll be fitter than this lot soon!"

The sailors onboard laugh. Even Arthur with his bloodied nose, prods one of the other men in his belly, jeering about how he needs to stop eating pies.

Although I am no safer than when I was captured, a weird sense of relief washes over me too. I remind myself that the Kingdom I see in the distance is not my home.

Far from it.

Kellan turns to his crew, "I could not have asked for better men. You served me well, obeying me no different than my father before me." His voice falters for a note.

The men offer quiet condolences, adjusting their momentary playful tone back to serious.

"Let us not forget why we embarked on this mission. May you never forget the importance of family. Once we've docked the ship, you are free to spend the rest of the evening with your families. Fletcher, you and I shall reconvene our meetings in the morning to discuss the matter of our family. Until then, steady as she goes."

"Steady as she goes!" The sailors respond in harmony before returning to their finishing tasks.

Sails are lowered, decks are swept.

There is a distinctive buzz in the air that we're almost there. That this ordeal is almost over. Although for me, this is just the beginning.

About half an hour later, the sunk anchor bites into the bedrock below and we slowly drift into the harbour. The citizens of Crescent Cove line the pier.

Without being prompted, some teenagers help secure the vessel whilst others line up the bridging plank to aid our dismount. Others standby and wave, hollering their hellos with beaming smiles.

Jealously bubbles in my core sending an acidic taste into my mouth. I would never be welcomed home like this. I doubt I would even be welcome there at all. Physically unable to spit, I am forced to swallow my own foulness.

The King grants permission for the men to disembark, and makes his way towards me, though he remained within grabbing distance for the remainder of the voyage.

He moves his body close and towers his additional foot of height over me.

He twists the knife into the tight knot that pins me to the mast and slices it in half. Ropes fall instantly and cover my feet, but I do not dare to kick them off.

I do not dare move. Mostly because I'm afraid my body will not respond to my request. My muscles are stiff. I think my joint have been replaced with chunks of coral.

Another much smaller part of me does not wish to move as the King presses the pointy tip of his blade against my chest.

"I thought about leaving you bound here for the night but knowing my luck you'd probably manipulate a shoal of coy from this bay to chew through your bindings," he says.

Coy don't have teeth, I think viciously.

Idiot.

"I offered you refreshment and an audience. I am a man of my word, but if you try *anything*, you will be going back out with the tide."

He does not speak it, but he makes it obvious he doesn't mean alive. The tension eases from the knife and he tucks it into the hem of his trousers.

He grabs my bound wrists tightly and walks in front of me as we step off the ship.

THREE

To evade most of the crowds, Kellen opts to haul me through the narrow winding streets. By avoiding the main town centre and market stalls, we only come across a handful of working locals. Each bow to their King and offer a smile, which some even extend to me.

As we approach the immense iron gates leading to the main castle, I slow my stride to take in the view, but he continues marching at the same pace. He merely shouts from a wide berth to the guard at the gate, requesting refreshments be brought after us.

He waits for no response; he simply trudges ahead with me in tow. We reach a steep stone staircase, to which he conquers two steps at a time. I barely keep myself upright as I stumble along. When I reach the top, heat flushes to my ears and I risk fainting my way down each and every step.

Noticing my struggle, he slightly smiles and nods towards a small cottage at the brow of the hill, "You're almost there."

A young woman jogs up the stairs and falls into step beside us. She carries a heaving tray, laden with cheeses, fishcakes and slices of bread, although she carries it as if it were a feather. She juggles the tray into one hand and opens the cottage door. Her perfect complexion and regular breath has me stumped.

Are the people of these islands mere mortals or are they mountain goats?

"Your Majesty," she says softly with a bowed head, "I have the refreshments you requested. Do you require anything else?"

Her fair eyelashes are so long it's a wonder she can open her eyes without effort.

"Thank you, Nessa. Just set the tray on the floor and you may leave us then," the King says simply.

She looks mildly stung by the lack of attention she was obviously craving. She lays the tray just inside the doorway, and quietly leaves.

Kellan throws me yet another threatening look before he releases his hold of my wrists and picks up the tray, "Follow me."

I wander after him at my own pace. The inside of the cottage is beautiful. Dense emerald carpet with golden swirls cover patches of cobblestoned floors, and large windows offer views of the harbour and distance sea stacks down below.

Kellan begins to arrange food and drink, before pulling out a chair for me to sit in. He unravels the rope confining my wrists, and flicks a finger at the syren bridle, "What are the chances of you bellowing like a banshee when I take this off?"

I concentrate on rolling my wrists and stretching my fingers, pretending I did not hear him.

He puts a firm hand on either shoulder to turn me around to thumb the clasps at the back of my skull.

We both stiffen as he slowly untangles the tentacles from my face. He leans close from behind as he reaches over me to place the clunky harness on the table. His warm breath catches on my neck as he remains behind me.

Still and steady, as if he's waiting for me to wreak havoc. So that's exactly what I do.

I draw a quick breath and release a long, slow note building in pitch. The narrow-stemmed glasses beside me vibrate and threaten to crack. The window rattles in its frame.

I wait to hear the King drop behind me, but instead a vice-like grip constricts around my neck.

"I think we both knew that was going to happen," he says sternly, sounding almost bored, "Knock it off."

Perhaps a single note wasn't enough to bring him under my control. I am out of practice.

Instead, I opt for a song I had learnt as a child. A simple but effective trancing lullaby ought to put him down.

With my rusty voice and tightening airway the song is horribly out of key, and to give the King his credit, I do sound incredibly like a bellowing banshee.

Instead of falling on his knees, he lifts me off the ground with one arm. He takes two steps and slams me against the nearest wall he can reach. My face is pressed firmly into the stone wall with such force my jaw clatters.

I choke into silence.

"Do you remember what I said about the tide?" he threatens quietly. Though a mere whisper in my ear, it's more unnerving than any roar I'd ever heard, "I brought you here so the townspeople would avoid the blunt of your abilities, but I don't need you giving them a blinding headache every time you open your damn mouth. If you're going to act like a bloody animal, then I will treat you like one. I could have you shackled at all times. Is that what you want?"

I'm aware he is waiting for an actual answer this time, but adrenaline is muffling my hearing. Panic is clouding my brain. I know I'm out of practice, but it should have worked. That level of singing that close?

He should be incapacitated and crying on the ground. Or clutching at his throbbing temples whilst fighting bouts of nausea; not pinning me against a wall.

"We can sit down like civilised humans and eat once I have your word you will behave yourself."

He shakes my collar slightly when I keep my lips sealed, "And don't think it's slipped my attention that you're avoiding my questions. We have studied your kind. I know you cannot lie, syren."

He keeps me against the wall, but I feel completely floored. How is it he knows more about my world than I do his? He knows I cannot lie yet I do not understand why he can withstand my abilities.

The familiar sense of urgency to run away builds in my core. Whether it's land or sea that incessant itch in my legs to flee never fully fades.

As much as I hate it, maybe I should have never swum away from home. My mother was right. I'll never survive on my own. For the second time today, I chastise myself for not feeling fear soon enough; it's always too late.

"Answer me, syren. Do you agree to behave?"

In my trapped position, my squished face is locked facing the tray of food.

Real food, not just some raw, scaly fish I sang to death. I'm famished for food and rest and have little energy to fight a battle I know I cannot win right now.

I try my best to clear my half-strangled throat and fully-fogged mind, "You have my word that I'll behave...whilst we eat."

Kellan hesitates, but releases his hold on me, "I don't appreciate you adding a time-span, but I guess it's a start."

When he moves his body away from me, my legs wobble unable to hold my weight.

I do not know the recovery time for kidnapping, but my normal rest time post-transition would be three days. I doubt I will get a mere full day here.

Not wanting to give him the satisfaction of seeing me faint, I quietly perch myself into the seat before me and hope I can eat my way back to full health.

The King pushes aside the carafe of wine with a look of disgust and instead pours himself a half glass of rum. He takes a slow sip, firmly crosses his arms and asks, "What's your name, syren?"

"*Syren this, syren that,*" I mimic his voice, although my voice crackles and creaks as it struggles to find its normal pitch. Weeks of not talking must have tightened my vocal cords...or maybe on some subconscious level I'm sick of talking back.

He shrugs as if the acid of my words has no effect on him, "It's what I'll call you until you tell me otherwise."

"My name is Wren."

"Just *Wren*?"

I shrug, too busy scanning the spread before me. I don't recognise most of the foods, and the ones I do seem too crunchy for my tender throat to deal with. I opt for the soft bread upon which I smear softer cheese.

Either he doesn't notice that I don't fully answer his question, or he just doesn't care enough to force it. Thank the gods for that.

"What age are you?"

"Seventeen." He looks a mere year or two older. Yet he is a King and I am a meagre hostage.

"Well, how long have you been seventeen then?"

"Nine months, one week and three days. I'm not immortal if that's really what you're asking," I spit.

"And where's your home?" He continues unphased.

"I do not have a home," I say sharply.

He raises an eyebrow but does not press the issue. Instead, he takes another sip of his drink, muttering, "*stowaway syren*," into his tumbler.

I pour myself a tall glass of pale pink wine and guzzle every drop. When I go to refill my glass, he judgingly swaps the wine jug for water.

On almost every smooth stonewall hangs a portrait of various royal family members. Most of them are strangers to me, but I recognise half of the couple depicted in the oil painting that hangs above the mantelpiece.

The man on the right presents the unmistakable features of King Lachlan. The crooked nose, raven hair offset by piercing blue eyes, and of course, his infamous scar running from his eyebrow to jaw. A reminder of his warlord days, and a clear message to everyone else that he fought to win the Lunar Lands. And he won.

I have never laid eyes on the woman in the painting, but I quickly establish who she is. With her wavy blond hair, high cheekbones and autumn hued eyes, she is the female version of the man who stands across from me. I feel his eyes on me, but I cannot pull my gaze away from the painting.

"I did not know Lachlan was your father."

He pulls an obnoxious face, wrinkling his nose in an ugly fashion, "Of course, he is my father. How else do you think I became King?"

"The same way Lachlan did. He stole these lands, killed the old King and appointed himself the new one." I shrug and reach for more bread.

Kellan lunges forward and slaps my hand, sending the bread flying across the room. It lands cheese side down. I try not to flinch as I hear my mother's nagging tone in my head complaining about the mess.

"My father grew his empire lawfully, challenging every ruler he encountered to a duel in combat of their choice.

He beat them every time. He always won. Yes, the original ruler would have been killed in battle, but Lachlan never harmed the citizens of the lands he captured. Do you not see how happy our people are?" His quick launch into this debate suggested it was one he had argued many times before.

I wondered if he won as often as his father.

"And how dare you suggest I would murder my own father," he rumbles, staring at the oil painting.

"Like I said, I did not realise you were his son. I thought all his children had perished."

He raises an eyebrow but lowers himself into the seat across from me, "Why would you think that?"

I hesitate under his heavy gaze.

"Tell me," he demands. It appears we've hit a trial he isn't willing to drop this time.

The magic in my blood, the part of me compelled by nature to tell the truth, sends a shiver down my spine.

"I often heard him pray to the gods across the sea. He questioned them as to why his weanlings did not survive. He would talk aloud to them as if they were all around, telling them of his plans or hopes. Other times he would just say their names over and ov-"

"I don't believe you." Kellan interrupts before sipping his drink and trying his best to look disinterested. He fails.

"You said yourself that you know I cannot lie."

"Faeries and nymphs always have a way of twisting their words."

"Don't you dare compare me to a damn nymph! If you do not wish to hear the truth then fine, but don't ask me for it then."

His eyes narrow as he decides whether he will tolerate being talked to like that. The room slips into silence and I consider singing once more.

I promised to behave whilst we ate, but he cut our deal short when he smacked the food from my grasp so...

"Fine then," he says suddenly, snapping me from my trail of thought. He begins tapping the inside of his ring finger against the side of his glass, "Amuse me. What names did my father call?"

"He asked the gods about Rhys and Rhett a lot. I think he referred to them as "*The Lazy Twins*"?"

Kellan smiles to himself, but there is something tragic about it, "*The Lazy Twins*" is a nickname he bestowed onto my brother Callum and I. We were born less than a year apart, and he always joked Callum was late, or maybe I was in too much of a hurry, always eager to be a leader."

Their playful nickname is a lot kinder than that given to me and my best friend Dove. My mother always referred to us as the "*The Typhoon Two.*"

"And what of the others? Callum?" I ask, shaking off memories of Dove and my mother from my mind. To spare a thought for either would hurt, but for different reasons.

"Rhys and Rhett were my other brothers after Callum. Rhys was born belonging to the Underworld, whereas Rhett was with us for a month before he slipped away.

Callum survived, he's eighteen now. He and my younger sister are all I have left."

I tilt my head, "Wait, Iseult is alive?"

Kellan winces, and his hand ceases its mindless tapping.

"No," he says quietly. He clears his throat and glances up at the painting, "Iseult is my mother's name. She passed away seven years ago giving birth to my sister, Aveen. How did you know her name?"

I consider staying silent again but I'm too tired to take another bout of his temper. Besides, it's my nature bound duty to dispense the truth, not shield people from it.

"Her name is the one Lachlan roared the loudest."

He doesn't doubt if it's the truth this time.

I thought it would be satisfying to hurt him, but it is not. The only thing I feel is a strong resemblance to my mother.

"That's enough," he says, as he scrapes his chair off the ground, "It's been a long day for both of us."

He moves behind me and reattaches the bridle before I have time to react. He tells me he is placing it back on so I don't wreak havoc whilst he's gone, but part of me wonders if it's because of what I said? If he is simply unable to hear anymore?

With more force than necessary, he hauls me from my seat, dragging me the short distance across the room. Plonking me on an emerald plush sofa, he once again ties an absurdly secure knot around my wrists and firmly tethers me to the heavy oak table leg behind me.

He leaves without saying where he is going, when he'll be back or what he plans to do with me. When the trailing sound of his boots on the gravel outside has fully passed, my imagination races to fill those answers.

I close my crying eyes and let the sofa take my weary weight. Being stolen from the sea, dragged into a boat and tethered like a beast is a horrible feeling. But knowing no one is coming to save you, knowing that even if I could escape, I have nowhere to go? That is the real cause of my tears.

I know nightmares are inevitable, yet I curl my feet onto the sofa and lie down anyway. With my waking life in such chaos, maybe for once the visions that haunt my dreams will be a welcome distraction.

FOUR

I'm home once again, safe inside the Water World of Seven Spikes, yet I do not feel at home. I most certainly do not feel safe.

Instead, it's as if I'm floating and drowning at the same time. Water surrounds me, but it feels too heavy. My body feels numb, as if it were too light. Every inch of this existence is unnatural.

Two mermen drag in a mortal being. The mermen have served the Queendom for over a millennium. Their immortal, unchanging faces are ones I could never forget, but this battered mortal is a man I have never seen before. The enchantment cast on him allows him to breathe temporarily underwater. Just long enough to serve his purpose.

A solid *thwack* from the merman's staff across the back of the knees crumples the mortal into a kneeling stance before me.

To my left is the coral throne upon which the Queen sits. Her ageless stare watches my every move.

I think about dashing to the right, but that side is flanked by Dove. The one face I'm grateful to see.

Her feeble, forced smile makes me want to cry. She is trying to be strong for me, for both of us, because as much as I don't want to do this, she is next. I always envied the mere five months between us. I never wanted the immortality side of this life, but I would give anything to pause time. To stop this moment and let her catch up to me. There is precious little I would not do in order to have her complete this ritual first. Selfish and cowardly, I know. But the tragic thing is, if Dove could take my place she would in a gill-flap. She hates our fate as much as I do, but she has always been the better friend.

The Queen gestures for me to rise, annoyed at my lack of forthcoming. Gripping the sides of my chair, I force myself upwards and float towards the mortal. With my tail taking up over four feet alone, I dwarf him. In my shadow, he looks petrified. I despise how powerful it makes me feel.

Gods above I cannot do this.

The Queen begins her hum. I normally loathe when she insists on being the centre of attention, but for once I secretly pray for her to upstage me, for her to sing the tune and not I. But she sticks to her mere humming tune. She doesn't sing at all.

From beside me, Dove joins in. She makes even a hum sound ethereal. Granted I have more ichor in my veins, and I am in direct lineage with Poseidon, but at that moment I swear she is a goddess herself.

She nods her silver-haired head encouragingly towards me. She was the one person I cared about, whose opinion of me I cared about, and she was about to witness me murder an innocent man.

No longer able to look her in the eye, I twist to find the unknown mortal man gone, replaced by a glower that remains the same regardless of location.

"Happy Birthday, *Princess.*" King Kellan spits at my feet.

I curl my toes and feel my guts twist. Pure hatred is all I see in his eyes, so I shut mine to block out the view.

"Do not keep me waiting," the Queen breaks her hum to warn me. It always bothered me that I can close my eyes but never my ears.

Swallowing the urge to cry, I muster up an ounce of courage to start my song, although nothing about this feels brave. Every part of this barbaric rite feels cowardly. I keep my eyes winced shut until I've fully finished the first chorus of the Lineage Lullaby. I need to make sure he is fully under my spell and in an idiotic trance before I continue. I cannot bear to look at him until he's mindless and-

Kellan clears his throat, "Problem, *Princess?*"

Shit. It's not working.

He looks at me with an angry yet bored expression, there is no trace of fear. It's almost as unnatural as me.

"Are you not strong enough to do this if I'm conscious, syren?" he asks.

I don't know which name I hate more, *syren* or *princess* but I chastise him for neither. He has the right to call me far worse.

Before I even open my mouth, the Queen shoves past me, blowing me to one side. She stands firmly behind Kellan.

Without pausing, she drives the Trident through his back until it bursts through his chest.

35

The centre prong pierces his heart perfectly. The other two do just as much devastation. His hatred filled stare remains locked on me even in death.

My singing is replaced by screaming.

With my jaw on fire from attempting to scream in the syren bridle, I lurch upright only to snag with my wrist restraints. My tears have caused the metal straps of the bridle to stick to my face. My cheeks are tight to move. I'm not in the Queendom, I'm in the cottage.

I'm no longer on Seven Spikes.

I'm no longer on Seven Spikes.

I'm no longer on Seven Spikes.

I tell myself over and over until I annoy myself into believing it. Nightmares are a regular occurrence, yet this felt in no way familiar.

Premonitions have not been part of syren life for so long the only cases I know of are ancient history, and even those tales are disputed to be the inner ramblings of ancient minds trapped in everlasting bodies.

Yet I know what I saw to be true. It was a warning; an omen not to be ignored.

FIVE

Conversation drifts into whatever half slumber I eventually succumbed to. Battling to open my heavy eyelids, my bleary gaze lands on Kellan.

He is altogether too close, squatting onto his haunches mere inches from my face.

"How the Hel did you break this?" he asks, somehow managing to lean even closer to me.

He reaches for something behind my back and without standing hands a shard of wood to Fletcher over his shoulder.

It's only then I recognise it as the leg of the table, which is now tilting to one corner behind me. Splinters lay scattered on the floor. Some are stuck to my skin. I swallow hard as the recollection of last night's omen drift back into my mind.

One of the few benefits of life undersea was no matter how hard I thrashed the waves around me there was never any evidence of damage. No harm is done to anything other than my sanity.

He reluctantly unstraps the bridle but remains within choking distance of me.

"I don't sleep well," I say, stretching my freed jaw. The King's eyebrows knit, dissatisfied with my answer. I ignore him and brush the wooden fragments from my body.

"On land?" Fletcher asks gently.

"Ever."

The King grabs me by the elbow and hauls me upright. He keeps a steadying hold for a beat longer than necessary, before he nods towards a bundle of fabric on the slanted table, "There are some clothes there. I guessed your size, so they may not be perfect, but they will most certainly be an improvement."

Both our gazes fall to the dark cloak I am still wearing as a dress.

"They'll do for now," he adds, finally letting go of my arm, "Shelli the tailor can alter them for you after the meeting."

"Wait, what meeting?" I ask, but he heads towards the door.

"We're gathering with the privy councillors to make a rescue mission plan for Callum and Aveen," Fletcher explains quietly, handing me the bundle of clothes.

Rescue mission? I hide my surprise, and instead shrug whilst saying, "Surely the plan is to get them back. Why does that take a meeting and councillors? Just get in a damn boat and retrieve them."

Fletcher tries not to laugh, "You sound like someone else I know."

"Hurry up," Kellan rumbles through the hallways.

"Speak of the devil," Fletcher grins and flashes a quick wink before leaving me to get changed.

Much to my annoyance, Kellan did a surprisingly good job at guessing my measurements. I fumble with the sand-coloured slacks, unsure as to which way they go on.

Trousers are not common in my world, and it takes me an embarrassingly long time to figure out the drawstrings go at the *front* of the slacks.

Thankfully the knitted grey jumper and soft leather boots are less confusing, although my face puzzles once again when I see a lightweight fabric remains on the table.

Where the Hel is this meant to go? I'm fully dressed. Examining the rectangular piece of designed cloth, an idea sparks in my mind. I catch the corner and pull harshly, release a loud *rip sound.* Much better, I think to myself, grinning with pride.

I find them waiting at the doorway once I am ready. Kellan roams his eyes over every inch of me. When his gaze loiters on my hips, my cheeks betray me and blush a light lilac.

"Don't flatter yourself," he says flatly, "I'm making sure you're not armed before I let you out amongst my people."

"Carrying a blade in one's waistband is your speciality, not mine," I retort, turning my pockets inside out for dramatic effort, "My weapon is not visible, yet infinitely stronger than any blade you could wield."

Kellan's jaw instantly pulls taut, "If you even-

"Look," I interject and close the minimal space between us, "Before you start another threatening speech to show off how big and bad you are, let me save us all some time. I have no intention of singing, and you have no intention of killing me. You said it yourself on the boat that you need me alive, so why don't you save your breath and explain why I'm here rather than your usual utterings of violence?"

Fletcher winces in the background and holds his breath, but neither the King nor I move.

He remains staring before his right hand flies up towards my face. I brace for him to hit but instead, he lightly tugs at the bow I fashioned in my hair.

"Is there a reason you shredded the brand-new scarf I left for you?" Kellan asks, before turning and making his way towards the table.

"Scarf?" I repeat, stumbling over the word. A name starting with *scar* seemed far too aggressive for such a patterned piece of cloth.

"The fabric you...utilised for your hair, it is normally worn around the neck during the winter months," Fletcher offers, with a guiding arm to follow.

"Kind of like a noose," Kellan adds pointedly as he yanks out a chair and then gestures for me to sit in it.

"Well I have no use for a noose nor a scarf, I needed a haircloth," I shrug, and straighten the bow I made to hold back my mop of inky curls.

"Inventive," Fletcher chuckles, as he makes his way into the kitchen. He returns with mugs brimming with steaming dandelion tea.

"Destructive," Kellan corrects. The King leans across me to retrieve two mugs. He sips from one and places the other in front of me with a thud, causing the tea to splash out the side.

"Thanks...I think," I mutter. He sits beside me and drowns his smug smile in his mug.

Fletcher bounces to his feet to fetch a rag from the kitchen.

"Why is your Master of the Sails here?"

"Fletcher is also my brother-in-law, so he has a right to be involved with the rescue mission."

"What is a brother-in-law?"

The King looks at me like I'm the dumbest creature he has ever seen. Fletcher thankfully has returned and is kinder. He mops up the spilt tea and is willing to stoop to my level of apparent stupidity.

"A brother-in-law is a male who becomes family through marriage, not blood. It's the title one gets after they wed a sibling," he explains to me, before throwing a look at the King, "We must remember what we studied about syrens. They do not have husbands or brothers. Our terminology is alien to her, your Majesty."

"And you must remember what I've told you about calling me 'your Majesty' behind closed doors," Kellan stands and shakes as if he has a wiggly eel in his shirt, "It's weird and makes me uncomfortable Fletch."

My mind reels as I untangle the web in my mind. Kellan said his mother died giving birth to his sister seven years ago...

But if Fletcher is his brother-in-law then he must have married Aveen. My widening eyes lock onto Fletcher and colour drains from my cheeks.

"What's wrong with her now?" Kellan asks, unrolling a map to cover most of the table. He starts scattering seashells in each corner to prevent it from rolling back up.

"I do not know a lot about mortal marriages or marriage in general, but that seems...wrong. Very wrong and unlawful and I...I can't," I lurch to my feet, struggling to string words together as bile rises in my throat.

Fletcher must be nearly three times her age. She's just an innocent child.

I turn my attention to the King and jab him in the chest, "And you? What sort of brother are you to allow it?"

Kellan smacks down my hand and steps closer to me, toeing his boots against mine. The unweighted corners of the map curl up. The rustle of paper is the only sound in the room.

"If you have such a problem with my brother and his husband, I'd be glad to escort you out of my Kingdom. Gills or no gills, I will drown you."

My brother and his husband? Fletcher is married to Callum?

Kellan stands so close the heat from his breath and the fire in his words brushes against my skin.

"I...I'm sorry," I mumble, wishing the sea would burst up through the ground to save me, "I thought he was married to Aveen."

Fletcher joins me in looking disgusted, but Kellan looks nothing but furious.

"What sort of King do you think I am? What kind of brother?" he demands

Fletcher slices his arm in-between us, "Calm down Kellan, she didn't know any better."

Unsurprisingly, he does not calm down.

"You won't harm me, will you?" Fletcher asks, his eyes sincerely begging me not to piss off the King anymore.

"No, I won't," I say, and gods above I mean it.

I'm normally not one to worry too much about other opinions of me, but I have an overwhelming urge to show him I'm not small-minded or judgmental. I consider telling him how in my world mermen always have male consorts but a small voice in my mind opts against it and I chose to stay silent.

"Tell her about the meeting, and if you need me, I'll be..." Kellan pauses to look me up and down, before stepping away, "Literally anywhere else."

He slams the cottage door with such force, the reverberations go through my teeth.

Fletcher and I remain still for a few minutes. Once he seems sure the temperamental King isn't going to barrel his way back in, he sits back at the table as if nothing happened.

"There is a privy council meeting this afternoon to discuss strategy on how best to attack the island, but it only seemed right to inform you of your role first. We do not wish for you to be bridled before councilmen, but the King will insist on it if you are likely to turn...volatile."

"Oh, I'm sure he'd love nothing more than to see me bound like some beast," I retort to which Fletcher offers a raised eyebrow.

I guess this is the sort of *volatility* he's referring to.

He straightens out the map and stabs a large lone island in the centre of the southern sea with a slender, jewelled finger, "Do you know what this is?"

I had never seen the unusually shaped island; it was further south than I had ever dared venture. Yet with its somewhat spherical core lined with long, sharp juts flowing into the sea, this magical looking land would be more suited up my neck of the sea.

"I'm a girl who lives by the sea, not in the air. I know not what the birds see," I muse. It never made sense to me why mortals depict their maps this way; as if they were approaching from above like Pegasus.

"This is Soleil Island. The ancestral homeland of the old shrivelled bore who used to rule the Lunar Lands before Lachlan took it. When Lachlan defeated him, his son Alastair sailed there the day after in hiding. Lachlan had no intention of slaying Alastair, who was only a teenager at the time, but I suppose his fears were founded. The Soleil Island and Lunar Lands had been a joint empire for centuries before Lachlan split it up. Over the years he reached out to Alistair, reassuring him that his land-grabbing days were behind him and he was satisfied with his Kingdom with no intention of expanding.

44

When Lachlan died four months ago, Kellan wanted to reassure Alastair that the deal still stood. A change in monarchs is always a time of great uncertainty. Kellan invited him to his coronation last month and to everyone's dismay, he arrived.

Kellan gifted Alastair numerous oil paintings of his ancestors which had been in storage for years, insisting the fights of their fathers should not become theirs.

It felt momentous. The new King of the North and the old Prince of the South in the same room. Alastair joked about how he might stay as he quite missed his old home, and Kellan mockingly joked about how Soleil island would make a nice garden for the Lunar Lands. Playful rivalry and nothing more. At least it's what we assumed.

That is until Alastair ripped Callum and Aveen from their beds in the middle of the night and stole them away to the south. He's held them hostage behind a fleet of patrolling ships and iron bars ever since."

"They were kidnapped from their beds?"

He nods sombrely, "Yes, but try not to repeat it around Kellan. He's having a hard time handling it. He's normally not as temperamental as you've seen him, but not having his family is driving him to some...unusual behaviour."

"Like capturing a syren?" I offer with a sarcastic smile. I can only imagine the blow to the King's oversized ego knowing his siblings were stolen from beneath his nose at his coronation.

"You were solely the King's idea. He woke one morning and started demanding we set sail to find a syren. I just followed orders. It seems rather silly to admit now, but I always thought syren's were a mere myth. Like elves, unicorns, or dragons," Fletcher confesses, shrugging one shoulder.

"Elves are most certainly real, but they're such bastards you're better off never meeting them. Unicorns and *Drakon's* are said to be extinct, but that's a lie. The Seven Spikes is a vast island with plenty of places to hide," I explain, trying not to smile when Fletcher pales, "Although I doubt Kellan would ride a unicorn to the rescue mission, and I doubt he would withstand a Drakon's abilities as well as mine."

Fletcher's eyes grow wide, "I'm assuming you figured out he can withstand your song by trying it? That would explain his moodiness about coming to the cottage."

"Why didn't my song work on the King?" I ask casually, trying to sound unphased, but my heart begins to sound like a spring tide in my eardrums.

If the King has come up with some ingenious way of blocking my magic, perhaps an herb concoction, then I can find a way to overpower it. Then I can find a way to change the omen.

There's an old hearsay that an iron tuning fork in front of one's chest helps to resist a syrens song. I always assumed it was complete codswallop, but maybe-

"He has ichor in his blood, not as much as you, but enough to make him resistant to magic abilities."

46

Fletcher halts my inner babble instantly.

Shit.

"How?" I ask once I've scraped my jaw off the cobbled floor.

"All of Lachlan's children have ichor. They inherited it from their father, who in turn got it from his father and so on, all the way back."

"Back to whom?"

"To Ares."

"Are you telling me Kellan is a demi-god?" I shriek. The yelp is not a syren sound but Fletcher whines regardless.

"Shh! Gods above, please don't say that, especially not to Callum. He does not need the ego boost. Demi suggests half, and they're nowhere near as potent as that. It's been diluted over the generations, although Lachlan and Kellan's thirst for war doesn't seem to have lessened. They are called Descendants."

Oh, the damn Descendants. Mortals with a god in their ancient history whose ichor still lingers through the bloodline. Technically speaking, syrens and other creatures are a type of Descendant though we would never call ourselves that. We were crafted by the gods with pure ichor and intention, not just the result of some mortal who fell into bed with a god.

"I thought most mortals could not carry children with ichor if they had none themselves?" I ask. Most of the gods had left a lineage line on the mortal realm at some stage through the eras, but with ichor and regular blood

47

being incompatible, those lines tended to fizzle out after a generation or two.

Fletcher winces and nods lightly, "It's not that they *cannot*, it just proves difficult and often ends rather ...regrettably."

I feel confused until I understand what he is saying.

Iseult.

Rhys.

Rhett.

"It won't be an issue for this generation. Kellan has vowed to never take a mortal wife for fear history would repeat itself. Children aren't exactly on the agenda for Callum or I. If Aveen wishes to be a mother when she is older, she already has ichor in her veins so either magic or mortal man would be suitable for her. That's if her suitor would survive the wrath of her older brothers."

The wrath of her older brothers. Wrath is right. Ares was notorious for his temper and impulsive actions, and I'm guessing that spirit is alive and kicking for these Descendants to still be around.

"If they have war in their veins why do they need me?" I ask.

Fletcher takes a mouthful of tea which is probably cold by now. He drums his fingers against the side of the mug, and shuffles in his seat, "Kellan plans to use your abilities to disarm Alastair's fleet. A syren is a powerful tool they won't expect us to have."

"I'm not a tool," I say sternly, "Nor a weapon."

"Of course not," he offers.

"And what is to happen to me afterwards? Once I have served my purpose? Am I to be discarded?"

Fletcher gapes his mouth open and shut a few times like a struggling fish. This cornered mortal could so easily lie to me, but his being stuck for words shows me he would prefer not to, "I do not know, I'm not even sure the King knows. But if you help me get Callum back, I will ensure your outcome is one which you desire."

The tragic thing is, I do not even know what I want. I learnt to stop wishing years ago. The closest thing to fulfilling a desire I ever achieved was running away and look how that turned out. I'm so used to someone else having command over my life that I do not know what would happen to me if I was given full control.

"Best we get going," Fletcher announces, heading towards the door, "Kellan hates to be kept waiting."

I roll my eyes and follow as slowly as possible. I get the distinct impression Kellan hates a lot of things.

SIX

Fletcher leads me down the hill and towards the tall iron gates I passed yesterday. The guard screeches one of the heavy gates open and wordlessly steps aside upon seeing us.

We make our way along the gravel path which stretches through the centre of the long lawn. Pathways are lined with bare trees and bland bushes, but I imagine this garden is beautiful in the summer months.

Every path through the garden leads to the castle which now stands before me. For someone with as big an ego as Kellan, I assumed his castle would have to be colossal to house it, but I was wrong.

The Lunar Lands castle is surprisingly modest. A square stone structure with a singular round turret on the right side. With most of the front walls covered in ivy, it looks as if it had not been touched in centuries, although a paler colour stone around some windows hints towards them being added at a more recent date.

A guard at the doorway directs us to the West Wing, where the meeting is taking place. The great hall is magnificent. A long centre table lined with velvet backed chairs, and a high ceiling made of wooden beams and glass. Long windows fill almost every wall, allowing bright, winter light into the room. It's refreshing...but I feel too exposed.

With so much visibility it's as if the gods themselves are invited to pass scrutiny. Although I would never admit it, I suddenly missed the cosy cottage.

Fletcher seats me between himself and Kellan. Nessa is putting the finishing touches to the wreaths hanging from seats, straightens the cutlery, and ensures each place has paper and a quill.

With as much judgement as a simple gesture can hold, she removes the knife from my cutlery set up and swaps the elaborate wineglass for a plain tumbler. She beams her annoyingly distracting smile towards the men as she fills the King and Fletcher's wine glasses.

"Shall I let them in, your Majesty?" She nods towards the closed double doors where the sounds of mumbling and shuffling feet are leaking through.

He gives a curt nod without looking up from the papers he's rifling through.

She gracefully twirls on the ball of her foot and heads towards the doors.

The second she turns her back; I slip from my chair and grab the decanter of rum from the nearby tray. Kellan immediately has his hard mouth half-open, ready to chastise me, but when I fill my tumbler with rum and set it down before him, he remains silent and curious. I snatch his wineglass by the thin, fragile stem and return to my seat.

Fletcher says nothing, but a comically raised eyebrow demands an explanation.

"He is the King, no one will question if he has a different glass. I am already being judged by everybody walking through the door, I do not need to feel like a clumsy child unworthy of finer things," I spit under my breath as the men begin to file in around me, "Besides, he doesn't even like wine."

"How do you know that?"

"I notice things."

Kellan is nodding greetings to the men, smiling and gesturing for them to take their seat once they've bowed. He does not look at me or acknowledge what I said, he simply lifts the glass takes a long sip of rum and clears his throat.

"Thanks." He mumbles so quietly I'm not sure if I imagined it.

With everyone seated, the meeting begins. Although I have no bridle constricting my tongue, I remain silent for the first hour.

I am meant to be the rarity in the room, the one people look at, but I cannot help but stare at the faces around me. I have never seen so many men in the same room at the same time. Normally when a poor stranded sailor is towed into the Queen's chamber, I never see him again.

The councillors argue amongst themselves as to what the best course of action is.

"I still think meeting Alistair at sea is the most feasible action, your Majesty," a man offers. His proposition immediately met with the groans of his fellow councillors,

"I understand my agenda is not the most popular amongst you, but I stand by it. In terms of time and coin, we cannot afford the other options-"

"At least the other option teaches the brute a lesson," a woman interjects.

There's a moment of collective nodding. Even the King seems to agree with her.

"Retaliation loses its appeal when you have to triple the taxes for locals to fund it," the man snaps back, before offering an apologetic bow to the King, "I'm sorry, your Majesty, but as Master of the Coin, my duty demands me to be candid. We cannot afford to strike the Soleil Island, and we most certainly cannot afford for you to claim it as your own. Under Alastair's rule, the island has amounted enormous debt we simply cannot carry."

"Master of the Sails, how is the shipbuilding coming along?" Kellan asks without offering any response to the other man.

Fletcher tries not to flinch under the deathly stare from the Master of the Coin, "Slowly but surely. We have completed the build of the new ship you commissioned. It has twenty separate cabins, which equals forty sailors if we do split shifts and sleep rotation. Work is underway to reinforce the bows and hulls on our existing vessels. Granted they're smaller, but I think they've proved themselves hardier than we thought possible when..."

His voice trails off, but he glances at me.

When hunting me? I want to add, but I hold my tongue.

"You still owe me for that bet by the way. I told you we'd be perfectly safe without an ice-breaker," Kellan leans back in his seat.

"Thankfully we won't require an ice-breaker in the Southern waters, but we will face other challenges. The Winter Solstice is in three days' time. It would be best to wait until after that to attempt the voyage. Our vessels would be too visible for Alistair's patrolling fleet. The fleet is also stronger than we first anticipated. A passing merchant told us to expect at least four to seven long ships each housing a full deck of men."

Kellan's face returns to its usual broodiness, "Hmm...what are my odds?"

Gods above, is everything just a game to him? Some contest for him to gamble upon?

"Slim, but this is where Wren comes in."

My spine stiffens at the mention of my name.

"You want me to better your odds?" I try to sound sarcastic, but it comes across more nervous, "What is it you plan on using me for?"

"That depends on what you're capable of," Kellan states, eyes locked onto me. This feels like a test, like he's purposely trying to provoke me into snapping.

If you're going to act like a bloody animal, then I will treat you like one. I can have you shackled at all times. Is that what you want?

Rolling my shoulders, I batten down the rising temper in my core. I will not sing here and paint myself as the monster he so wishes me to be. I am capable of restraint as well as chaos.

I prop my elbow on the table and rest my chin atop it, "I do not wish to insult your Master of the Sails, but you have it all wrong. Winter Solstice is the best time for the voyage. A powerful, bright moon will give me a higher tide to pull from. The stronger the wave, the stronger my attack."

I pause to hear their response but there is none. The councillors just glance at one and other silently.

"That is what you want me for, right? My attack?"

I shrug, stand from my chair and move closer to the wooden model of the Soleil Island.

I select a handful of intricately carved boats to symbolise Alistair's fleet, "You can cease reinforcing your boats. I'll disarm the patrol fleet alone. Once they're out of the way, you will have a clear path to the harbour. But I will have to get out of the main boat around here," I say, setting down a figurine a couple of inches away from the main island, although it will be a couple of hundred feet in real life, "And I'll swim this distance alone to ensure my song does not also affect the Lunar Land sailors."

"Would you really require *that* large a buffer area?" Fletcher asks, paling a little as my abilities register in his mind. When I nod, mumbles and gasps ripple throughout the room.

"You don't honestly expect us to release you into the sea, and simply hope you stick to your word of swimming forward alone to attack? What is to stop you diving away and abandoning us?" The same woman as before demands to know.

I told myself I wouldn't sing but the temptation to hurl a figurine at her head is overwhelming. I place both wrists on the table and lean closer to her, "If anyone in this hall should have trust issues, it's me. I was plucked from the sea to fulfil this isle's requirements. I am offering to bloody fulfil them, and you will not trust me to do the task at hand! I'm not in the business of reassuring people who have kidnapped me that I'm worthy of their confidence-"

A bell chimes through the room. Its high-pitched ring echoes off the walls and silences everyone, including me.

"Time for lunch," Kellan interrupts, waving a golden bell up and down. Before I get another word in the doors swing open and servers file in. Trays of food and fresh bottles are placed in rows along the table. With their greedy eyes scanning the dishes before them, no one is even aware of my presence anymore.

I slump into my chair like a child.

Kellan pops an olive into his mouth, "I didn't want you losing your temper."

Oh really? I think it's exactly what you wanted.

I snap a breadstick in half and pretend it's his arm. Is this what I'm like on mortal soil? Full of swinging moods and emotions? Or perhaps the King's presence just brings out the worst in me.

Nessa waltzes in with a basket of dried fruits on her arm, and a small parcel for the King.

56

"This just arrived via seagull, it seemed important," she offered with a nauseating smile before bouncing away. Yes, bouncing, like a hare.

Using his trusty knife, he slices open the parcel. He glances inside before immediately stiffening.

He swallows hard, before dropping the envelope as if it burnt his fingertips. His grip on the knife tightens until his clenched knuckles turn white.

"What is it?" I ask quietly, not wanting to alert the others to the King's sudden stillness, although most people are busy eating or chatting amongst themselves.

He uses the tip of his knife to nudge the parcel across the table, not wanting to touch it again.

I hesitantly peer inside to find a golden tunic clasp, covered in a mysterious, violet-hued liquid which had dripped and smeared across the inside of the paper.

"My mother collected pins and brooches of every kind from every island. This is the one she was wearing when she perished. My father gave it to Aveen when she started school. She used to wear it in her hair. I doubt she gave this up easily," he says, sounding physically pained.

"What's the liquid?" I almost whisper.

Without explanation, he squeezes his palm around his blade. He does not wince. It is terrifying and tragic how unreactive to pain he is.

He opens his palm to me under the table to avoid an audience. Blood pools in his palm but it's not the regular shade his sailors or privy councilmen would have, that mortal men should have. Yet it is not the same sapphire shade as mine either.

A deep mauve liquid drips from his fist and splatters on the floor. The same colour as that on the broch.

I've seen a lot of mysterious things in my life, but never this.

"Our mother was a mortal. She had crimson blood like every other person on these isles. But Lachlan's blood more closely resembled yours. His ichor mixed with her blood to give the three of us this bizarre purple-hued mixture."

"A blend of mortal and magic," I say quietly, setting down the parcel now I understand his anger. He was right in his guess that she would not give up her mother's clasp easily. My mind race with thoughts of the terrified, and possibly tortured princess.

No home.

No hope.

To me, it's a rather familiar and poignant issue.

"This is not a false threat from Alistair. This is Descendant blood belonging to one of my siblings. I just pray it is Callum's. At least he's old enough to take a beating."

He wipes his hand on his jacket, ruining the embroidery, though I doubted he ever wore the same thing twice.

He shoves his chair back but pauses before standing, "I know what it's like to hide behind an ego. The shield of bravado is often hard to lower, but I need to know if you are capable of disarming the patrolling fleet the way you said."

"I cannot lie," I say flatly, feeling my temper bubbling up once again.

"You should not be that powerful." He shakes his head in disbelief

"Yet I am," I say, and before he asks me how, I add, "You wanted me for this very reason. I want to get your family back for you, but I cannot better your odds if you don't trust me."

He mulls over my answer with a face he normally reserves for drinking rum. He straightens himself, tucks his knife away and clears his throat, "Attention."

The room falls instantly silent. People pause mid-chew. Everyone focuses their interest on their King.

"We set sail for Soleil Island on the Winter Solstice. The new ship will house a strong crew of our best sailors, and that will be enough. There is no need for the smaller boats, but ensure a single rowboat is stowed for the voyage, I will need it to approach the patrolling fleet with Wren."

I don't know whose outcry is louder, mine or Fletcher's.

"You cannot come with me," I splutter.

"With all due respect your Majesty, is that really the greatest idea, or even a safe one?"

Fletcher keeps his formal tone, but his facial expression is a different case. We all knew behind closed doors later he would be far less polite.

"She cannot hurt me. I am immune to her abilities," Kellan says.

"She broke Arthur's nose just fine without her song," Fletcher reminds him.

I stick out my tongue, but he does make a valid point.

"I'm deciding to trust her," Kellan says firmly. Half the room look at him, the other half at me, but after that, no one questions him further, at least not at loud anyway.

As he goes about setting tasks and readying his men, he looks every bit the King he was raised to be. Orders are handed out; plans are drawn up and before long the entire island becomes alive with energy.

"Finish stuffing your face, we set sail in three days," he says to me before turning on his boot-heel and vacating the hall.

I stare at the spread before me, but I've forgotten what it's like to have an appetite. With knots filling my stomach I doubt I'll ever feel hungry again.

SEVEN

Three days later, a knock arrives on my cottage door before the sun has even begun to rise. I open it to find a cautious Arthur. He stands about ten feet away from the door, but even with the distance and grey dawn light, his blotched, bruised nose is visible.

Before I figure out why he is collecting me instead of Fletcher or Kellan, he politely nods before wordlessly walking towards the dock. I guess I cannot expect him to want to chitchat with me. I leave a lingering touch on the cottage door before jogging the few steps to catch up to him.

Half the city has come out to see the men off. The other half have come to see the brand-new ship. It's an impressive vessel, and larger than any other I have seen in the Lunar Lands or anywhere else.

Upon seeing me, most of the crowd move aside. I drop my gaze, not needing to see the disgust and fear on their faces so early in the morning, but a little hand pulls on my trousers.

I barely lift my eyes from the ground to see the young child only reaching to my knee.

"Good luck," the dainty girl announces before trotting back to her smiling mother who's waiting a few feet away. The mother offers a gracious wave before bundling the child into her arms to give her a better view of the ship.

Once I've managed to pick my gaping jaw off the cobbles, I realize the crowd around me are not retreating from fear, but from respect.

My path is paved with smiling faces and well-wishers. Gods above, do they even know what I am?

Various voices holler out *"Safe journey"*, *"May the gods protect you,"* and one person even shouts, *"Sing loud and proud, syren!"*

Huh.

Okay, so they do know what I am, they just do not seem to mind.

As we reach the end of the pier, I crane my neck towards the countless sails above me. They waft in the winter wind and cast shadows on the deck below.

Along the deck, dozens of sailors stand in neat rows awaiting Kellan's attention.

He moves slowly through the lines, greeting each man by name and shaking their hands. On each of their foreheads, he marks a circular shape using a pot of ash and his thumb.

"What is he doing?" I whisper to Arthur as we make our way onto the wooden plank to board.

"The King is offering them a Phoenix Blessing, it's an old pirate ritual. You take the last spare plank from the building of a new boat and burn it. You anoint each crew member with the ash so they may have part of the vessel in their veins. They will feel a changing tide faster, recognise the boat's needs and become one with the sails.

It ensures a safer voyage," Arthur explains with great pride as he steps on board.

Fletcher offers an outreached hand to help me take the last step into the ship, "Good morning."

Once I'm steady on my feet, I expect him to let go but he holds tightly onto my hand and even pulls me slightly closer, "Now don't freak out but, the consensus on board is that you should wear your bridle."

If looks could kill, he would have dropped dead at my feet. There goes my fleeting idea of the Lunar Lands citizens had accepting me as a syren.

"Did I not prove myself at the privy council meeting?" I huff.

"You barely held your temper in a hall full of diplomats for an hour or so. These men are the ones who found you, so they know what you're capable of. Being surrounded by your source of power?" He gestures wildly to waters around us, "It's putting them on edge a little bit."

Arthur strolls past as if he can't hear every word Fletcher is saying, but I catch his sideward glance when he pretends to busy himself with nearby ropes. He looks away quickly, but I see reddening cheeks merge into his blotchy purple nose.

"On edge a little bit?" I ask, speaking loud enough for everyone to hear, "Nothing is stopping me from singing right now. I could have you all under my spell before you've even undone a strap on your bloody bridle! How dare-"

"Wren." The King doesn't shout the word, yet it rises above all other sounds.

"What?" I snap.

It's my first time talking to him since the meeting, but it's already too soon.

He simply offers a raised brow which threatens to smudge the perfect ash circle in the centre of his forehead. He gestures towards the cabin door and waits for me in the doorway. I march over with my hands on my hips and skid to a halt.

"I'm willing to trust you, but you cannot expect the same from the sailors. I would place less faith in you too if I knew the damage you could inflict with a single tune."

Harsh but true.

"They're frightened of me."

"Yes," he says coldly, even though it was not a question, "And I will not force them to be nice to you, it would be a waste of time and a disservice to everyone involved. But I will ask you to wear your bridle when on this ship."

He hands me the device. The weight of the iron and decision feels heavy in my hold.

"What if I don't want to?" I challenge.

"I could make you," he warns, "But I won't. I meant what I said. I will try my best to trust you, but you must respect my crew. It is not a question of if you want to, it's a matter of need."

When I do not respond, he simply shrugs and anoints my forehead with ash.

"I'm the latest daughter in a long line of syrens, created by Poseidon himself. I am one with the sea. I have little need for some pirate prayer," I announce, throwing my eyes to the heavens.

He glides his thumb down from my forehead and slips it under my chin, forcing me to meet his gaze.

"It's a wonder you don't have swirls in your irises from rolling your eyes so damn often. You're still part of this crew, regardless of how high and mighty your great grandfather might be."

He turns his back to me and returns to the deck, leaving the door wide open after him. I kick it closed, sit cross-legged on the bunk and remain clutching the bridle. I stay there for the rest of the day.

"We're about to eat if you wish to join us out here," Fletcher's voice rumbles through the door a few hours later.

I stare at the door and answer him with silence, hoping he knows I'm actively ignoring him and not just asleep.

Another two hours pass before the door blows open.

"Out," Kellan says devoid of any emotion, "You can continue to sulk if you must, but do it on the main deck. This cabin is needed for the sailors."

A timid looking sailor stands behind his King. He offers an apologetic smile as I move to my feet.

I pause beside him in the doorway.

"Rest well," I mumble, before putting on the bridle.

Across the ship, chores are being swapped and delegated as the first rotation takes place. Half the men will rest, whilst the others maintain a steady course and keep alert for the first signs of Alistair's fleet.

I find an empty, long bench at the base of the mizzenmast and occupy myself with watching the sunset.

An array of colours I'd rarely seen, dance across the shimmering waters. Shades of saffron, scarlet and peach flicker like droplets of flames, threatening to burn the waves. But before long, the sea gets its way and appears to swallow the sun just beyond the horizon. The gods paint the skies above us a twilight grey, and the men around me drape themselves in black cloaks.

I thought this ominous shift would unsettle the men, but instead, they become more alive. Candles and lanterns are struck a light, and old-fashioned pirate ballads are lightly sung in rhythm with their rope heaving. Apparently, not all songs sung upon the seas are detrimental.

Apart from me, the only other people refraining from the jolly melody are Fletcher and Kellan. Fletcher is at the helm, keeping a firm grip on the wooden wheel. To his left is Kellan, plotting out routes on a large map using a small compass and the faint, emerging stars above.

They do not sing like the rest of their crew, the only words passing their lips are about the mission at hand. They meticulously go through every detail of the operation repeatedly, planning backups and outcomes for any possibility.

It's all mundane and rather tedious to listen to until Kellan asks what the plan is if he and I were to continue to Soleil Island alone.

"Why on the seven seas would you do that?" Fletcher asks, taking his worn-out eyes off the waves for the first time all day.

"There's a chance we might have to if I fear Alistair rushing to do anything reckless."

"Reckless?" Fletcher almost shrieks, "You said yourself Alistair was a coward. All talk and no action. That is why we left them with him for so long. If you feel like he might be reckless than we should have stormed this blasted island weeks ago!"

Long gone were his notions of adding '*your Majesty*' for appearances sakes. A vein bulges across the centre of his forehead and is shadowed by the candlelight. I thought containing such a temper was an ability solely for me. And perhaps Kellan.

"Well I tried to set sail after them the night they were taken and what did you do? You locked me in a damn wardrobe," Kellan snaps back in a hushed tone. Probably because he doesn't want the men to hear about their strong King getting held in a clothing cupboard.

"I locked you in a wardrobe for your own protection. You were drunk and furious, Hel-bent on slaughtering Alistair with your bare hands. I could not let you leave when you were out of your mind."

Kellan's eyebrows slam down, "You think I wanted to kill him because I was drunk? Fletcher, I wanted to end him because he took our family. I still want to end him."

"The councillors said-"

"I do not care what the councillors said. They are also the ones who advised against me syren hunting, yet I still went."

He glances at me and I suddenly find the grain in the wooden bench fascinating. I bury my eyes into the grooves and lines, tracing them over and over to appear too busy to be eavesdropping.

Although from the way the sailor closest to them is repeatedly winding and unwinding a length of rope, I doubt I'm the only one catching an earful.

"When it comes to protecting the people I love, there are no rules decreed by any man nor god that I am not willing to break," Kellan says firmly.

Fletcher sighs and seems to soften, returning his gaze to the waters, "I know you will do what needs to be done, but promise me sailing ahead without the fleet is the last resort?"

Kellan pats his shoulder, "It's Plan Z, my brother."

For the rest of the night, they swap stories of Callum. Kellan shares a lot of embarrassing childhood tales, whereas Fletcher tells of drunken misadventures and wedding mishaps. Although they compete for the most mortifying stories, their love for Callum is palpable. His body may be held captive on Soleil Island, but it feels as if his soul is right here with them.

I unfurl my back along the bench and stare at the constellations above, wondering what it is like to have people who would stop at nothing just to have more memories with you.

EIGHT

The sailors who were worried about me being surrounded by the sea got something right, there is an increase in my magic. Although it is not an effect I desire. My mother's voice and the background hum of the sea rings louder here.

Sleeping blocks out some of her noise but lends itself to another source of misery. Before I even realise I've nodded off, the nightmares find me once again.

This time I'm swimming frantically away from the Seven Spikes. My tailless legs are thrashing the currents, kicking up water in a trail behind me. My arms ache as I force them to chop through the waves, propelling me forward with as much speed as possible.

A strong urge to glance over my shoulder creeps in, but I bat it away. No good ever comes from looking back. Focusing on the horizon, my wide eyes lock onto a lighthouse in the distance. If I can get there, then I will be safe...at least I think I will. I swim harder than syrenly possible, yet the distance does not shrink. I get no closer to the shore.

"Is something the matter?" A distant voice laughs from behind.

It's only then I notice a rope tied around my waist joining me to her. I catch the slack and pull hard, yet nothing gives. My mother would not be Queen if she gave up easily.

"I do not know why you're always trying to swim away. You are mine," Her voice grows closer, but I do not look behind me.

I tell myself to look at the lighthouse, to only focus on the horizon.

"I *always* will find you, all it takes is a little..." Her voice trails off into eerie silence.

I break my own rule. Turning around, I find myself alone in an expanse of sea. Maybe she did me a favour and drowned?

I twist at the hips, scanning the waterline in every direction, but she is nowhere to be seen. The seas are clear, the horizon is safe and the lighthouse...is gone?

I blink four times and look again. But it has vanished.

My heart begins to race, pounding in my ears and thumping against my chest. My chest which is now glowing, bright and steady with each passing heartbeat. My radiance lights up the waters around me, splattering golden flickers across the waves just like the sunset.

"What are you doing to me?" I scream, my trembling hand afraid to touch my torso.

"All it takes is a little fear," she finishes, emerging from the waters before me, "Your fear makes you a beacon. I hear your ichor rushing through your veins."

I try to slow my breathing, to appear in control and brave, but the glowing does not stop. My lighthouse heart illuminates her dark face.

"I told you, you are mine and I will always find you."

I bolt upright, almost falling off the bench. One hand grabs the rail to steady myself, the other reaches for my chest. The fabric feels damp from a mixture of sweat and sea spray but there is no glowing light.

It was just a dream; I tell myself as I straighten my bridle and smooth out my sleeves. I struggle to take a handful of long, deep breathes through the syren bridle. I could take it off but at this moment I feel as if it's holding me together.

I'm not sure if there was any truth to my nightmare, but I still try my best to ease my racing ichor. It turns out forcing yourself to relax is a futile effort.

Instead, I distract myself by watching the sailor complete another shift rotation. Fletcher hands over the helm to a newly awakened Kellan. Arthur is completing his handover to another sailor by showing him various points on the ropes and sails.

He's gesturing to something halfway up the main mast when his eyes drift to the dark waters overboard.

"Is that...a dolphin? Some sort of sea lion?" he asks the other sailor.

"I'm not too sure but there's three of them," Fletcher says as he begins his tired walk to the cabins, "They've been tagging along for hours, weaving in and out under the hull. Playful little things."

Any trace of sleep drops from Kellan's face as he takes a few strides to the edge of the boat and inspects the spectacle.

"They're not seals or dolphin. They're hippocampi," he declares flatly.

My stomach drops. Syrens do not ever feel seasick, but I imagine this is what the ailment resembles.

You are mine. I will always find you.

I glance down to make sure the lighthouse heart has not materialised, because if my racing ichor is a beacon then every inch of me should be ignited.

The deck is momentarily abandoned as men, including Fletcher, race to the side of the ship to get a better view. Although I don't know why they would want to. They are more terrifying than they are exquisite.

As the chattering sailors begin to wake up the other men, I find myself get caught up in the thrill, and for reasons unknown, I look over the damn boat too. One of these days my curiosity will kill me.

I understand now why the men mistook the species. With their heads and hooves busy breaking the waves, only their rear is visible. The long scaly rump leads into a tail resembling that of a dolphin.

Without warning and in eerie unison, the creatures snap their long faces up and look directly at me.

Seawater drips off their dorsal manes. Their expressive, black eyes are wide. Their nostrils flared, as they gallop through the waves to keep up with us. To keep up with me.

"They're a magical creature...Why would they be this far south? It's unheard of," Arthur asks with an enthusiastic tone that makes me want to vomit.

"Perhaps they're hunting for something" Fletcher offers, ever the logical sailor and scholar.

But these creatures are not well documented for a reason. Any mortal close enough to recognize the sea beast normally didn't live long enough to write it down.

More like hunting *someone* than *something,* I mentally correct.

I push away from the edge having seen enough. My eyes drift across the bare deck to find Kellan has remained by the helm. He leans against the wooden wheel and stares at me. Intensely.

Turning on my heel, I make my way towards the sleeping cabins, which are all vacant now thanks to the overboard entertainment.

If only they knew.

Kellan pushes himself upright, tucks his knife and hipflask into his waistband and follows me into the cabin.

"Acquaintances of yours?" he accuses with a flat tone. He catches my wrists and holds me in the doorway.

I snag them away and point to the bridle.

"I'm surprised you haven't taken it off so you can belt out an inviting lullaby to those beasts. I know hippocampi are messengers for the Water World."

He's half right. Hippocampi are the most common heralds of my world, but he got one thing awfully wrong. There is no way I could control to those beasts. That was always my mother's speciality, not mine. Never leaving her Queendom meant she had to master the skill quickly to maintain her tyrant like presence far and wide.

I know little about hippocampi except they are rarely a good omen and I have a strong disdain towards them. I know not of their aural abilities, but I swear they were listening to every word Kellan just spoke, as on queue they deliver their tidings.

Each wails a different insult, but they all mimic the same voice. Her voice. A mutated tone of my mother's tongue rings all around me.

"I allowed you your time to be a stubborn brat, but you have strayed too far, Princess. Return immediately."

"Quit frolicking around the seas. Your duty is here."

The men gasp in awe. Of course they do. All they hear is the unusual hybrid call of a hippocampus. The extraordinary symphony of clicks and neighs echo across the water, but all I hear is taunting.

"Did you really think I would not find you?"

I crumple to my knees and slump my back against the wall.

Cradling my skull in my hands, I rock myself back and forth, but the self-soothing motion does nothing to aid my pain.

"Taking an Ares princeling as a consort? I did not expect that of you. Do not think you will ever rise above me."

Kellan stands over me. His stature filling the doorway. He does nothing but watch me squirm beneath him. I guess he's relishing in it. It's the closest to bowing he'll ever receive from me.

He withdraws his knife.

I would normally react, either flinch or brace, but I cannot. I can't do anything but listen to their contorted cries. If he wants to stab me for being the traitor he deems me to be, then fine. At least it might bring some relief.

He drops to my level and wordlessly slices the closing clasp at the back of the bridle. In a single motion, he slips it from my face and tosses it far across the room. Some of the metal octopus tendrils bend and shatter from the impact.

As I predicted, the second my lips are free they form a scream. The noise in my head is debilitating. The pain it causes is all I focus on. For a fleeting moment, it seems to be getting quieter, or maybe they're retreating underwater as the sound becomes muffled. I raise my fingers to my ears only to find them damp with blood and ichor. The sound is not decreasing, she has just damaged my eardrums.

"You always have, and always will be, a disappointment," squelches in my ears.

Kellan steps over me and reaching for the decorative harpoon nailed to the wall. Pulling it down, he inspects the bladed tip. It's sharp enough to momentarily cut the screams in my mind.

"What are you doing?" I hiccup, using my trembling hands to wipe tears from my eyes.

He leaves my side, takes nine long steps and takes aim over the side of the boat.

"Where are they weakest?" He shouts back at me over his shoulder. A dozen wide eyes turn to stare at me.

There's no way he would be able to hit it from a moving boat. Even if he did, surely slaying one of her messengers would just infuriate my mother more. Although I don't know if that's possible.

"Wren," he roars.

"Their flank," I croak.

The meld of wet fur and scales runs in a faint line around the lower gut of the beast, and it's the sole place of vulnerability.

He draws his arm back far, and in one smooth arch, fires the weapon overboard.

I cannot see if he strikes the creature, but gods above I hear it. The strangulated whinny erupting out of the hippocampus is a clear signal he struck its Achille heel. The raucous noise is loud enough to drown out the cruel chattering in my mind.

As the injured beast fights to stay above the waves, the rest of the herd dive deep below. Their cries mercifully dissipate with them.

The sailors immediately snap their attention back to their King, standing upright and proper.

"There are other harpoons throughout the ship. Gather them and keep them at hand. If they resurface, you shoot," he says flatly, "Actually, kill any creature coming within spitting distance of this fleet."

"Yes, your Majesty," Fletcher says without hesitation or questioning. Even though they are friends and family, he knows when to take an order. He knows when not to talk back.

I wonder how long I would have to spend with him for that trait to rub off on me.

I crawl into the cabin and do not look back as I kick the door shut. I eye the bunk before me but cannot find the energy to haul myself into it, so instead, I stay on the floor.

I do not dare to sleep at sea anymore, and I most certainly do not peer over the side of the boat.

I sit and wait for Kellan to knock on the door, demanding me to give up the cabin, but he does not come. I do not leave. I'm not sure I could face him or any of the crew after that. So why do I wish he could knock on the door to check on me?

NINE

I do not talk to the King again until we're being lowered into a small rowboat off the side of the main vessel. We had travelled as far as we could as a unit, but with Alistair's patrolling fleet coming into view on the horizon, the time had come for us to continue alone.

Kellan gave strict instructions to the men before we left. The sailors were to wait until every boat belonging to Alistair has been disarmed. All the men agreed and quickly got to work without delay. Well, everyone except Fletcher.

His spirits had plummeted almost as fast as their anchors. As he handed the King the oars, he muttered, "I should be going with you."

"Her song would obliterate you," Kellan said coolly, seemingly unaffected about sitting across from someone he deems so dangerous.

"I could use her bindings and strap myself to the boat. There would be no luring or throwing myself overboard, that way."

"Ropes might prevent the physical symptoms, but your mind would be frazzled within a single note," I explained, "You would no longer be the man Callum knows and loves."

Fletcher paused.

Kellan gave me a raised eyebrow, apparently grateful at my ability to strike a chord with Fletcher. Harps, lyres, human heartstrings, I play them all.

We row for about an hour before Kellan asks, "Should we have waited for nightfall? Would the cover of darkness have been better?"

To strike first and think of strategy later proves he really is a Descendant of Ares.

"Day or night makes no difference to my singing. I'm neither a morning lark nor a barn owl," I laugh without humour, "Besides, they've already spotted us."

The ships a couple hundred feet ahead are now drifting in a slow turn to face us and closing the space between them. They think forming a wall will protect their fleet, but it's a grievous mistake on behalf of their Master of the Sails. The poor bastard doesn't know he's just making it easier for me to strike.

I set down my oars, move to the helm of the rowboat and stand on the ledge.

"Do you wish to commandeer their ships for your islands?" I ask without looking back.

"No," he says after a beat, "The only thing I care about right now is my family. I'll pillage the scraps once I know they're safe."

Great, that makes my job a lot easier.

Reaching to the sea, I submerge my arms until the waves tickle my elbows. As if it were a blanket, I slowly lift out an armful of water.

Kellan gasps behind me. Who knew he was capable of being surprised?

I lift the captured wave towards my lips and whisper a simple chant. With an almighty push, I fling the wave back to the sea and watch it race towards the boats. It breaks against the side of the first vessel, releasing my words for the sailors to hear.

"*Ela se ména,*" echoes across the waters.

Come to me.

It's the simplest of luring mantras but also the most reliable.

Obediently, sailors from the first vessel frantically clamour over each other in a race to fling themselves overboard.

If the solid *splat* against the wall of water they smack into did not kill them, the icy winter waves should.

With the first ship's wheel no longer being turned, the vessel drifts uncontrollably towards the long vessel beside it. The collision is slow-paced and rather anticlimactic, but it's enough to penetrate the side of the other boat. The splintering wood and groaning hulls joins the symphony of screams.

The stronger willed men who have remained aboard the other boats are next. Some of them are already convulsing on their knees, gripping the mast to avoid jumping overboard.

If I paused for a moment to think about what I was doing I wouldn't be able to continue. So I do not falter, I cannot afford to. I compel myself to continue before they have time to regroup. I part my lips, tilt my head back and serenade them into the sea.

It is not a tune I have ever sung myself, but it is one I know by heart. It's the melody of choice for the Queendom if any fishermen trawlers were deemed to be too near. It was the closest to a nightly lullaby I ever received.

Failing sails float downwards. The billowing canvas spreads out across the water, trapping whatever resilient souls have yet to perish beneath its skirt as if it were a suffocating jellyfish.

It's pathetic how much relief it brings me not having to watch their flailing arms splash around.

Coward, I hear in my head. I'm unsure if it's my mother's voice or my subconscious.

Holding my tune, I glance over my shoulder to make sure the Lunar Lands fleet is far enough back to not be affected, but my eyes drift to Kellan instead.

He has moved to stand behind me, completely unaffected by my power. His weapon happy hand is resting on the hilt of his sword, but he does not have it drawn. We both know my defence is far superior to his right now.

I want to tell myself most of the men have just swum behind the jagged rocks and jutting out landmasses peppering the Soleil Island coastline.

I want to pretend I have not massacred dozens of men in a handful of minutes without laying a finger on them.

I want to act as if the rush of power doesn't set me alight, that this moment isn't the most in control I have felt in years. But alas syrens cannot lie, not even to themselves.

The sinking ships disperse the choppy waves which rock our little rowboat. When my already shaking body wobbles, Kellan wordlessly wraps an arm around me, yet he does not pull me back into the boat. He holds me steady, allowing me to look outward towards the chaos I have caused.

My song breaks as it turns into sobs. Gods above what have I done?

The last two boats drift away with the current, allowing the distant pier to come into view.

Kellan grips my waist tighter than usual, and for a beat longer than I'm expecting. I cannot tell if it is an act of solidarity or if he's simply worried I may fling myself overboard. It would be a lie to say the thought didn't cross my mind.

before he lightly releases my waist and sets about lowering the oars in the water once more.

"What are you doing?" I ask without hiding the fact my face is tear-stained.

"We're continuing ahead. I need to get there before the rest of our fleet arrives."

Though I feel no mortal temperatures, I'm still surprised to see him shed his cloak. He folds it in half over the bench and sits on it. I may not be able to feel the cold, but he sure as Hel should. He turns his back to me and begins rowing. His back muscles ripple behind his white shirt which is taut from the work.

"What happened to that being *Plan Z?* You cannot just skip most of the alphabet to suit yourself," I spit.

"I knew you were listening."

"So what if I was! I heard you promise Fletcher going ahead alone would be a last resort. You promised to wait for them."

"I may have ichor in my blood, but not as much as you. Not enough to bind me to the truth. I lie sometimes, Wren."

His rumbling voice fills the rowboat, and although I do not condone her actions, I'm beginning to understand why my mother murders every man she meets. They're infuriating.

He continues, "The advisers I have on the privy council want my men to capture Alistair and bring him before a trial to determine his punishment. They think Soleil Island is a resourceful isle we need to realign ourselves with through some Treaty."

"And?"

"*And* I plan on holding a funeral, not a trial," he says flatly, "If my councillors deem the island is so resourceful than I'll capture it as my own. Soleil Island and the Lunar Lands were always meant to be a unit."

"Have you not taken enough? Enough lives? Enough land?" I snap, gesturing to the floating driftwood and sinking bodies around us.

"I know you hate me for making you do this, but I will not stop until my family is returned to me. No price is too great to pay, no man is too important to kill, no land is too arduous to capture. I alone will determine what is enough."

He's right. I do hate him.

I fling the oars forcefully to one side, then cross my arms tightly in front of my chest, "I'd appreciate if you could stop hauling me off in boats to islands that I do not wish to visit."

It was not a joke, yet he smirks anyway.

My protest against rowing remains, but I do eventually concede and offer a silent, strong wave to help propel us forward. Anything to help us get through the debris faster. I cannot stomach the sight.

My supportive tide leads us to the Soleil harbour in no time, much to Kellan's delight. I am far less delightful.

"Is there any hope of you staying here?" Kellan asks as we close the narrowing space between us and the harbour.

"Not unless you tie me to the boat again," I shrug truthfully, "Although there is a chance someone could steal me before you return, being on an island with a ruler known for kidnapping and being a stolen syren and all that."

He mumbles a curse in an old language that would make the even older gods blush.

As we approach the pier, he does not slow the boat, nor does he even attempt to lower the tiny anchor Fletcher gave us.

Our boat collides into the wooden pier, snapping two of the planks and cracking a hole in our hull.

"Make me an oath then," he says calmly as our boat begins to take on saltwater, "Swear you will not leave my side."

I blanch, from his suggestion and his actions. I didn't know which is crazier, writing off a perfectly good boat or expecting me to bind myself to someone so unhinged.

"I will do no such thing! What if I were to get held prisoner or someone *finally* kills your annoying ass, then.... then..."

"Then what happens?" He elegantly pounces from the sinking boat onto the broken, slimy pier but his step doesn't falter.

I scramble onto the wooden ledge but go no further. Seawater floods into the boots and splashes against my ankles. Maybe I'm better off just sinking with the boat.

"Oh, do your little books not have that part?" I spit, "The ichor in my body would be bound to uphold its duty of remaining by your side. If we were separated it would try to leave my blood to stay near you, and I would die...painfully. There are faster ways to dispose of me once you're done using me as a battering ram."

Citizens who have heard some of the commotion have made their way towards the harbour. I say *some* of the commotion because if they had heard it all, heard the gurgling screams of their men and the destruction of their naval fleet, they would have run the other way. It was only I who had a suicidal level of curiosity.

I refuse to meet his stare, instead, I focus on the bubbling waters rising above my knees.

He wraps a solid arm around my waist and yanks me onto the pier and into his hold. Using his free hand, he withdraws his blade and points the tip at me.

"Promise that you will *return* to me."

He says each word slowly and with a calculating tone as if he fears I will find some loophole.

"Have I not proved myself loyal? Have I not conquered those boats for your benefit?"

Someone in the gathering crowd hollers our way. The last thing we need is an audience and we both know it.

"Promise me, Wren," he urges in a husky rasp.

I ignore the way my stomach twists when he says my name.

"Fine, you have my oath. I will return to you, King Kellan."

There is a pull in my core as the binding words take hold, and for a moment all I think about is vomiting on his stupid shiny boots.

"I hate you," I declare out loud, mostly for him to hear but I want to hear it too.

I need to. I need to know it's still true because I'm not so sure anymore.

Somehow satisfied, he hands me the knife and wastes no time in storming towards the castle grounds. With the murmuring crowd looming and the last bubbles emitted from the sinking boat behind me, I abandon the sea and take off after him.

TEN

We hoped sailing ahead alone would maintain some element of surprise, but apparently, news travels faster than us in Soleil. By the time we reach the castle gardens, a man I assume to be Alastair is waiting in the middle of the gravel path. Along with a lot of bodyguards. Thankfully most of them small, the rest of them somehow smaller.

Fletcher had described Alastair's father as an old bore, and I see now the pearl didn't float far from the oyster.

His face is so bland I worry if I took too long blinking I might simply forget who I was talking to. The only remarkable thing about the southern Prince's face was how truly unremarkable it was, and the overwhelming look of fear he tried to bury beneath his smug smile.

"I see your father's habit of waltzing onto islands uninvited is somewhat genetic," Alistair says.

Kellan subtly thumbs his cloak to reveal his knife, "I inherited a lot of skills from my father.

The bodyguards immediately draw their weapons, but Alistair raises a grandiose hand to pause them.

"I'm assuming you came all this way to plead for your siblings' release?"

Kellan allows the fabric to fall from his hold and crosses his arms with as much indifference as he can display, "I've never pleaded for anything, let alone from someone so...lesser."

When the bodyguards take a step closer, I place a grounding hold on Kellan's arm.

"You're letting your Ares side show," I mutter.

"Good," he rumbles.

"And who's your *little* friend?" Alistair asks Kellan directly. His emphasis on my stature immediately causing me to stand up straight and cross my arms.

"I'm the one who singlehandedly destroyed your entire navy," I retort. I say it without pride, but it comes across malicious regardless. I guess there's no polite way of using it as an introduction.

The Prince raises an eyebrow but remains silent. His gaze shifts from Kellan to me and back again.

"You know, I initially felt terrible for stealing away your young sister. I was not much older than her when I was ousted from my home, but looking at you now..." Alistair pauses to wave a pointed finger between the two of us, "Now, I believe this isle may be the safer haven for her. At least here she is locked away from such vile and murderous monsters."

The songs I sing are meant to be the most terrifying sound one can hear on this side of the world, but the growl erupting from Kellan's chest comes a scarily close second.

"Bring. Me. My. Siblings."

The Prince flinches, and it takes everything I have to not do the same. Even if I am not the intended target, standing this close to Kellan when he's this furious is daunting.

Alistair nods to two guards on his left. They turn in unison and march off to fetch the prisoners.

"Your family will be returned to you under the assurance the islands which were once my fathers are reinstated to me. The Crescent Cove, Meteoroid Spit and Star Spike all rightfully signed over to rightful heir," Alistair says, tapping his chest with a pointed finger, "The Lunar Lands are my birth right, but Lachlan stole that from me. When I was invited to your farce of a carination, I assumed you were going to reinstate my title and give me back at least, some if not all, of my rightful isles, but no. Instead, I was expected to sit back and watch *my* crown be placed upon your head! I could not understand it when all around me people applauded for you. You? You are nothing more than a self-righteous, trespassing orphan. You are nothing."

To our equal surprise, it's me who lurches forward, not Kellan. He remains where he stands but he grabs my forearm, his vice-like grip threatening to shatter the bones beneath my skin.

"Do not get too close to him. I fear the very air around him is tainted from his toxicity," Kellan says flatly, "Alistair, let me make this simple enough for even you to comprehend. You can bend your knee, or you can lose your head. The choice is yours."

Immediately the guards tilt their weapons forward in a collective smooth motion.

"Oh, piss off," I spit, "A herd of new-born seahorses would be more intimidating, you bunch of-"

The advancing crunch of gravel stops interrupts my train of thought. The guards have returned, dragging a shackled Aveen and Callum in tow.

Just like his brother, Callum's taller stature means his head is visible above the others, even in its drooped state. He does look remarkably like Kellan; the nickname of *Lazy Twins* suits them well. Except Callum's cheekbones are not just high; they are forlorn and gaunt. He has his brothers chiselled jawline too, yet his own looks far too angular, too harsh. Just skin stretched paper-thin over bones. Stubble dabbles across his jaw, greying his already pasty skin.

Aveen, on the other hand, takes after Lachlan. Her dark hair is pulled into a messy braid trailing down her back. A thick piece of dried seaweed keeps her plait in place. Deep purple circles encompass her young, yet exhausted eyes. Eyes which suddenly gain a sparkle when they land on Kellan.

"I told you he'd come!" she cries to Callum. She attempts waving our direction, but the iron shackles keep her hands firmly weighed down.

Dried blood, laced with ichor, stains her soft skin leaving vein like trails from under her shackles to her elbow.

"Why is my sister shackled?" Kellan roars with a heat that could melt the ground frost, "Those restraints are for a man four times her size. Are you really that afraid of a young girl?"

It's a rather smart insult, undermining Alistair's ability to fight off a child whilst also making him look malicious. I had to hand it to Kellan, he was good at handling anger. It did not cloud his mind like it did mine.

Alastair huffs, "Lady Aveen is not just *any* young girl. She's the sole daughter of Lachlan. Rumour had it he had his first blood at nine, so why would I leave it to chance that his daughter would not best him?"

"And what age do you think the eldest son of Lachlan had his first blood?" The twisted smile pulling at the corner of Kellan's lips is utterly terrifying, but for some reason I find myself smirking along with him.

"Just know the next blood I spill will be yours, and the land on which you stand will be mine."

Alistair gives a nod to his men, who immediately move into a circular formation around us. Standing back-to-back with Kellan, I eye the guards' bladed staffs that are pointing right at us.

"Give him the Lunar Lands. We'll sail south and seize new lands. No plot of rock is worth your life," Callum hollers.

"My life is in no danger here, brother," Kellan chuckles into the face of the guards, "As Wren said, they're as scary as baby seahorses."

A guard lurches forward to attack, but Kellan catches his staff and uses it to yank him forward.

"Weren't you told to piss off?" he questions.

He snaps the staff in half over his knee, the sudden release blowing the guard back off his feet. Kellan swings the splintered around the circle, pointing the sharp shard at every man.

"Now!" Alistair shouts at his men.

The circle surrounding us constricts fast, but not as fast as Kellan's arm around me. Squeezing me against his torso, he spins slowly whilst keeping a wide eye on everyone around us. He swings the wooden staff towards the men, viciously maintaining the mere two feet of breathing space we have left.

Sharp prods from their bladed tips come in at every direction, although Kellan is taking the brunt of the stabs into his back.

He cranes his head over my shoulder and presses his warm, damp lips against my ear.

"On *three*, get Aveen out of here," he growls quietly. His body jerks as the attack continues to rain from behind. I twist to see Callum using his shackled hands to scurry his sister behind him as best as he can.

"How the Hel am I meant to get to her?" I shout, not getting on board with the secretive whispering plan.

"*Two*," he warns.

Shit, apparently, I missed *one*.

"*Three!*"

Kellan lunges the broken staff straight through the intestines of the guard before us. He crumples to the ground.

Before I have a chance to take in the sight of pooling guts and splinters, Kellan roughly flings me towards his siblings through the gap he made.

I land in a pile at Alistair's feet, splitting both my knees open on the gravel. I glance up just in time to see Callum's elbow collide with the Prince's nose. A spray of hot, red blood mists my face.

"Save her!" Callum shouts. He gathers the slack chain behind his arms and as best as he can with constricted mobility, whips the metal across Alistair's face.

I scramble to my feet and scoop the scarily frail Aveen into my arms. I run a few strides, but her kicking and wiggling within my hold makes progress near impossible.

"Let me down!" She screams at a pitch that makes my head spin, "I won't leave them."

Her wide blue eyes frantically flit between her brothers. Callum and Alistair are rolling around on the ground fighting and Kellan...

My heart drops from my chest and lands somewhere in my stomach, hitting every organ along the way.

Bodies surround him.

Some are dead, but most alive. The living guards grapple with their clawed hands to snatch a hold of him, or simply stab aimlessly in his direction. Even the deceased guards are a hindrance as he stumbles over their corpses, taking up the precious ground he already had so little of.

Through the chaos, he catches my eye as I set Aveen down and step away from her. Even from here, I see the hatred in his eyes. He believes I'm abandoning them and leaving this fight.

Well, he's half right. I am leaving this fight, but I will not abandon them.

Without picking a particular song, I begin to sing. It's a rushed note which starts off way too high-pitched. It would surely make other syrens cringe, but it will do for the task at hand. The clang of weapons grows momentarily louder as staffs and shields are dropped onto the gravel below, but then silence.

One by one every guard ceases their fighting. They straighten, turning their attention to me.

Aveen looks herself up and down, wiggling her fingers to make sure she isn't under my spell. Callum shucks off a mesmerized Alistair and tries desperately to catch his brother's eyes for reassurance, but Kellan's gaze is still locked firmly on me.

My voice finds it path and I begin the same "*Ela se ména*" chant as before, but there is one crucial difference this time.

The message of my chant is not carried the distance by a controlled wave. There is no sea between us for my song to lure them into. There is no time-delay or ocean buffer. There is just them, me, and the mere dozen feet of gravel between us.

One of the hypnotized guards' lurches forward, breaking away from the circle surrounding Kellan. Once he moves, the momentary stillness is shattered. I spin on my heel and bolt away. Sprinting as fast as I can, I waste no time looking back. I do not need to. The clamouring boots and hasty yells from the men lets me know they are right behind me as if they are tethered by some invisible rope.

Zigzagging through the gardens, I try to lose some of them along the way, but the task proves futile. My magic has commandeered their minds, turning them into persistent moths to my stupid flame.

Pumping my arms and legs to maintain a safe distance between us, my body begins to fail me. Syrens were not designed to run, and these guards are startlingly fast.

Now heaving for breath, my song starts to fall apart, my hold on the men begins to unravel. I no longer lure them towards me, but my magic has done its damage. Some are chasing because they lust for me, some will desire to murder me, but *all* will have an overwhelming urge to hunt me. They will not stop until either they succeed, or their hearts stop beating.

Clutching hands grab at me as I round a tight corner only to find myself at the base of a stone staircase leading into the next tier of gardens.

Great.

It's only about a dozen steps but it might as well be Mount Olympus.

I bound the steps two at a time, but I'm only halfway when my left leg is nabbed mid-air.

A vice-like grip on my ankle yanks hard and sends me soaring backwards through the air. I'm swiftly dragged back down each stony step. A cry escapes my lips as the abrasive rock scraps at my back. My soft skin splits over the bumps of my spine.

I'm dumped in a pile at the base of the stairs and roughly flipped over to see the fastest guard towering over me.

With his frazzled mind, he no longer knows *why* he wants me, only that he does.

His overly dilated pupils leave no room for a coloured iris. His eyes are nothing but black. His crooked smirk resembles no smile. There is nothing friendly about it. Just sheer delight in his triumph. He was the fastest. In his broken mind, he won the hunt. He won me.

Gods above, he makes Kellan's kidnapping of me seem like a favour.

The brute wraps a thick palm around my neck. It feels impossible to sing when the urge to scream is barrelling through you, but I must. My lungs are now heaving so hard against my chest I worry they may erupt, but I somehow draw a strangled breath.

I scream a fragmented note. My desperate cry echoes against the stone wall behind him. He turns slowly, like a dumb Giant, conflicted by which sound to follow.

I waste no time in kicking my leg upwards and landing a dull punt between his thighs. He crumples sideways on the ground which slows some of the other men who have caught up and are trying to knab me next.

Finally reaching the top of the steps, I take off sprinting into the wide plain with a vast view of the sea before me.

In the distance, I see the Lunar Lands fleet closing in, but it's still too far. It will take too long to get to the harbour and it's time we do not have. I would be able to swim the distance but exhausted Callum and Aveen would not be able. If their brother had not wrecked the rowboat that could have been an option.

Think Wren, for the love of gods, think!

I sprint across the damp grass, kicking up clumps of earth in my wake. Ahead to my left, I see Callum and Aveen stumbling up another set of steps.

"Get out of here," I yell, fighting the urge to look back. The mob behind me growing ever closer.

"He said to follow you," Callum roars across the distance, "He said you'd have a plan."

Huh, so it turns out Kellan can be wrong. I thought it would be more satisfying to learn this, but figuring out the bloody plan I'm meant to have it the only thing I've time for in my mind.

A hand snags my elbow and yanks me back. I twist to see a toothless guard smiling at me, trying to caress my hair.

"You're so beautiful," he soothes, leaning in to kiss me with fully black eyes.

Pale hands catch either side of the guard's head before his neck snaps violently to the left. He drops downward, leaving a panting Kellan standing in his place. A thin slit runs down his face from his eyebrow to the corner of his lip.

"Run," he demands, grabbing my forearm and tugging me after him.

"Go wait in the harbour for Fletcher, they're on their way, I can-"

"We can't," he says flatly, "All the streets are blocked. The entire town is making its way towards you. There's only one way to the boats."

He storms towards the cliff, yanking me as my feet dig into the grass below.

"We cannot do this!" I shriek, eyeing the drop to the sea below.

"We cannot do this *without you*," he corrects.

Callum and Aveen skid to a stop at the cliff edge and peer over the long drop. Choppy waters and jagged rocks pepper the water below.

"Whatever you're thinking, do it now," Callum grates, staring at the second wave of guards and townspeople who are beginning to pour into the garden from every step of steps.

Shit.

I harness the surge of panic in my core and turn it into something useful. Gathering what little energy I have left; I throw my arms wide and call forth the sea.

It grows fast into a furious wave, rushing towards the cliff. I summon another one to chase it, somehow even larger and faster than the first. Together they merge to form the wall of seawater, cresting at almost thirty feet high.

It slaps against the coastline and threatens to swallow this island whole as it splashes over the cliff edge. It retreats as if it's taking a deep breath. As if it's preparing to swallow us whole.

"Get ready," I scream over the wave, over the pandemonium from behind, over the chaos in my mind.

Kellan scoops Aveen up and swings her onto his left hip. As he takes a stride back, he does not look at the violent waters below. He does not glance at his screaming sister in his arms who is trying her best to kick him.

He just keeps his jaw locked; his stare fixed on the horizon.

"I know you can do this, Wren," he says with an unnerving calmness.

As my wave returns, I empty everything I have into it. I pour my energy into it until I become the wave. I am one with it, it ebbs and flows within me.

I ignore the spots clouding my vision and instead pull harder, commanding the water to return to me once more.

The waiting feels like an eternity, but then the wave responds to my plea and suddenly it feels all too soon. The largest swell I'd ever seen rushes towards us.

"Now!" I roar, not believing I'm even uttering the word.

There is nothing left except the sea rushing to meet us. Kellen doesn't pause to enact a grain of common sense. He simply flings himself and Aveen off the cliff and into my tidal wave without a second thought. Callum squeezes his eyes shut and flows suit. I unlock my knees and step off the cliff.

My towering wave absorbs our hurdling fall and cushions our landing. My cry of relief releases the power, allowing the wave to die down. It rapidly sweeps us out to sea without a chance to look back. I know if I were to look back, I'd see men running off the cliffs only to land on the rocks below, and that is not something I can witness after the destruction I have caused today.

The clamouring of swords, roars of men, racing boots all gets left behind, but one scream stays with us.

Aveen's terrified cry bellows across the sea the second she resurfaces. Her mop of dark hair has come loose from its braid and suffocates her face in wet thick clumps.

Kellan bobs up beside her. He winces as saltwater saturates the slit across his face, but he shakes it off, immediately turning his attention to his sister. He pushes the mountain of hair out of her eyes and runs a soothing hand across her head, "Shh, it's alright Aveen."

"He...he followed us into the water," she sobs, wiggling her small frame around in Kellan's arms. Her lip quivers uncontrollably as she scans the sea over and over again.

"Alistair?" Callum asks. He's barely treading water, the weight of his shackles leaving only the tips of his shoulders and head above water, yet he upholds a façade of calm for his sister, "He will never hurt us again."

I swim closer and without hesitation or permission, wrap an arm around Callum's waist and help him paddle along. He stiffens immediately under my touch.

"But how do you know? Dad always said there were creatures in the bay, but I just couldn't see them in the water, what if Alistair is down here. He could grab my feet and-"

"Aveen," Kellan says firmly, placing a thumb under her chin and guiding her worried face to his steady gaze, "Alistair is dead. Beheaded. He is never coming for you. Either of you. No one hurts you and lives."

He turns to nod to Callum, and it's only then I notice the stain across the front of his wet shirt that clings to his toned torso. Blood has soaked through every fibre of his shirt, probably stained his skin beneath too. It now leeches into the waters around us.

My heart automatically lurches for a split second, but then I remember his ichor. This crimson smear is all Alistair.

The relief I get when I know he is uninjured is worrying. Almost as worrying as the way Aveen beams at her murderous big brother and leans against his bloodily chest unphased.

"Is that...?" Callum's croaky voice reverberates through his rattily chest, too thin to house any muscle, nothing to muffle the sound.

Four heads twist to see the trailing fleet come our way. Fletcher stands on the bow of the nearest vessel and gives a slow, wide wave.

"Fletch!" Aveen cries excitedly and almost leaps from Kellan's hold.

Thanks to my immense wave pulling forth so much water, the ship arrives within minutes. Ladders are quickly thrown over the side. Aveen is passed up first and immediately wrapped in an oversized grey blanket.

Callum is singlehandedly hauled into the boat by Fletcher. Before his feet can properly hit the deck, he immediately plants a sloppy kiss on Fletchers winter chapped lips.

Sailors whoop around them playfully, and Arthur lets out a loud whistle before leaning over the ladder.

"Do you need any assistance, your Majesty?"

Kellan pauses on the first rung and glances back to find me frozen in the water. I'm used to the bitter temperatures. The waters surrounding Seven Spikes are liquid ice, yet I cannot move. I'm rigid. He takes one look at me and knows this is nothing to do with the cold.

"I'll be there in second, Arthur. Ready the men, we're all going home."

Arthur vanishes out of view and there's nothing left in this moment but Kellan and me. He reaches out his hand and gives a beckoning nod towards the ship.

"I...I can't."

His eyebrows instantly slam downwards, "What do you mean?"

"It's not my home," I say with more jealously leaking through than I intended. I stare at Aveen, swaddled and surrounded by loyal sailors who might as well be a dozen brothers. How different my life could have been if I was a princess to the Lunar Lands and not the Seven Spikes.

Even half-starved Callum already looking healthier as if Fletchers kisses were nutritious.

Gah.

Stupid happy family.

"You told me you don't have a home."

"I don't...but that doesn't mean I don't have somewhere I should be."

Kellan mumbles something under his breath about syrens and their damn mysteriousness, before reluctantly releasing the ladder and closing the space between us with a single stroke.

His lips are almost as blue as mine. He may be a Descendant, but he can still succumb to hypothermia.

"Get in the ship. I'll need to bring my family home first before I can accompany you on any voyage. We'd need more supplies and-"

"You cannot go where I am needed."

He wraps his grip around my wrist and urges me towards the ladder, "Well then you are not going. Either we go together, or not at all."

"I don't need a damn bodyguard."

"Oh, I'm aware," he muses, shoving me up the ladder towards the sailors above, "You've just shown me how strong you are. How brave and capable. The reason I won't let you go alone is not because you need protection, it's because you're mine."

"Your protection or your syren?" I ask, landing on the deck with wobbly lands. A kind sailor breaks away from the group huddled around Aveen to hand me a similar grey blanket.

"Both I guess," he muses, vaulting himself over the edge of the boat to land right behind me, "But more importantly, you're my friend."

I'm not cold but I wrap the large blanket around myself anyway, needing to have another layer between us. Anything to make him feel less close.

As he pulls his brother and Fletcher in close, tousling their hair and joyfully slapping their shoulders, I slip away to my cabin.

I need to be away from all this happiness.

I need to be away from him.

"Keep an eye on her," he says loud enough for me to hear across the deck, "Make sure she doesn't try to fling her overboard again. I have no intention of letting her slip away."

ELEVEN

I return to the same cabin as before and do not remerge. I sit in solitary silence, but I do offer a helpful tide to help get us back to the Lunar Lands faster.

There's a rhythmical knock on the door as the last drop of light comes through the circular window above the bunk.

"Wren?" Kellan calls quietly outside my door. I expect him to barge in, yet he doesn't.

"I'm going to tuck Aveen into bed and watch over her for the night. Callum said she's developed nightmares whilst on Soleil Island. I'd hate for her to start snapping table legs."

I laugh slightly, before quickly covering my mouth.

He waits a beat before adding, "I know you hate me, and I apologise if what I asked you to do has caused you any distress. I'm just letting you know I'll be off the deck, seeing as you cannot stand to be in my company. Goodnight Wren."

I push myself off the bed and cross the room. My hand wraps around the door handle and swings the door wide open, but he's already gone.

I look down the corridors to find them empty. At the bottom of the hall, a door quietly closes.

Sighing, I make my way onto the deck, aiming straight for the food table.

Fletcher is peacefully asleep against his husband's chest. Callum's skinny arm drapes over him, holding him tightly.

I pop a few dates in my mouth, grab an apple and spin on my heel to return to the cabin.

"Wait," Callum says in a loud whisper.

When I glance over my shoulder with a high eyebrow, I see him beckoning me over with a single finger.

I pace my way over and shrug before him, "What?"

"Can you hand me the jar from the table? I'd get it myself but…" He lightly shrugs the shoulder supporting Fletcher. It's a relief to see him peacefully sleeping at last. Granted, it's on a slim bench on the deck instead of a cabin, and even with his eyes close Fletcher keeps a limp hand on the wooden steering wheel, but it's a start.

I hand Callum the large glass container, filled with what appears to be sea cucumbers and rum, "What the Hel are these?"

"Pickles," he whispers, and pats the sliver of space of the bench beside him, "Sit, and have one with me."

"Eww. No thanks."

"The pickle is optional, the sitting is not," he says soberly, "I want to talk to you, and thank you."

"Do not thank me," I say flatly, opting to remain standing. My request is not one of humbleness.

If I accept his gratitude, then I'd feel like I had an option, or did a favour. I simply did what had to be done, and that's the only way I'll ever be able to live with it.

He gives me an arched eyebrow, and pats the bench once more, "Alright, we'll just talk then. I've never met anyone like you"

"A syren?" I huff, crossing my arms. I'm far too tired to be a source of weird and wacky entertainment.

"Don't get me wrong, being a syren is interesting," he mutters quietly, tapping the bench again, "But I'd prefer to know more about *you*, Wren."

"Alright then, I'll bite," I sigh and sit beside them, taking a bite out of my apple for dramatic effect, "What is it you want to know?"

"Well, we'll start with an easy one. What do you like to eat?" He shrugs towards my apple.

"I mostly eat fish of some sort. If one of the girls is performing her Luring Lullaby, I normally scour the ship for produce."

"Luring Lullaby?" he repeats to himself, "Is that what you learn about in your school?"

"*School?* Please tell me you did not just refer to me and my fellow syrens as a *group of fish!*" I accuse him in as loud a whisper as I can muster. I grip the side of the bench, readying myself to leave.

"What? No, no," he says, shaking his head, "School is what we call our lessons and studying."

Oh.

I try to batten down my temper and take another bite of my apple to give myself time to think. I don't think I'll ever seamlessly fit into this realm, especially with their confusing terms.

"We spend most of our time preparing for our chants and lures. I guess it's the only real *school* we have," I offer, "But you said you wouldn't ask about syren life, but instead *me* and *my* life."

He holds up his free hand apologetically, "Of course. So, answer me this, why do you have such disdain for my brother?"

A cocky grin spreads across Callum's face as I drop my jaw.

"I...He...You know he kidnapped me, right?" I stutter, shaking my head in exasperation.

"Ah, you'll get over it. How do you think my father met my mother?" he laughs coolly, enjoying watching me squirm, "Pickle?"

He points the open jar of slimy-looking sea cucumbers towards me, and although I despise even the scent of them, I accept one. Anything to not have to talk about Kellan.

I take an overambitious bite which causes my face to contort from the sourness.

Callum chuckles, "Get used to it, most of our vegetables are preserved in vinegar to survive the winters here."

I take another, much smaller bit, unsure if I loathe it or not, "How do you eat this whole?"

Callum pops one straight into his mouth and flashes a cocky wink, "Oh if you think it's impressive, wait until you see Kellan's ability to demolish a whole jar single-handedly. He likes things deemed acidic by others."

"It's ironic he dislikes me then," I muse, flinging my pickle over boarding, having enough of it and this conversation.

"I don't think-"

Callum is cut short by the flapping sail overhead. Loose ropes whip around the deck as the wind picks up. Fletcher wakes up immediately without being prompted. Perhaps the Phoenix blessing worked; it's as if he's one with the seas.

Seagulls and harpies squawk overhead. Towering waves begin to lap against the side of the boat. One would easily dismiss the sudden turn in tides as a winter storm, if it were not for the hippocampi cries only I understand.

I will always find you, rings through one ear and out the other. I whip around, expecting to see my mother behind me.

You will return to me!

Hearing the echoing cries of the beasts once more, Fletcher lurches from Callum's hold, springing to action, "There are harpoons at the back of the deck, and more in the cache cabin. Wake the men and grab Kellan, he'll have to take aim again!"

"What's going on?" Callum demands, looking frantically between the harpies, Fletcher and me. But he receives no answers.

I press my trembling, middle fingers against the tragus of each ear, and with wobbly legs make my way towards the back of the boat.

"Wren!" Fletcher shouts over the wind, "Get into your cabin!"

I release my right ear, using the hand to select a single harpoon from the pile. Using it as a steadying staff, I climb onto the ledge and try not wobbly off balance.

Leaping fish breach the choppy waters surrounding us. Jellyfish slap their tentacles against the boat as they clamber towards me. The hippocampi momentarily pause their galloping to drop back to the rear of the ship and wait for me.

With nausea bubbling in my gut, I twist on the balls of my feet to face the deck.

A flustered Kellan rounds the doorway but freezes when he sees me. His face hardens instantly. He's barely awake but already fully aware of what I'm about to do.

The harpoon is not heavy, but my shaking arms struggle to raise it high. I draw a shaky breath and aim directly at Kellan. He freezes in place, shouting something at me but I can't hear him. I think it's better this way.

I told him I would save his family, and I will keep my word. I will not entice the sea and all its creatures onto this boat. They have a family to protect, and a home to get to.

I have nothing to lose. I have nothing.

I give him a weak nod before dropping the weapon and allowing myself to fall backwards into the sea.

He lurches forward, but it's too late. I smack the waves below before he can even get close.

As the choppy seas pleating around me, the harpies descend. They wrap their wings around their bodies and spin rapidly downwards, penetrating the waves effortlessly and sinking to a depth of twenty feet.

The hippocampi fall silent.

The leading stallion swims over and lowers his neck in a submissive fashion. I grip onto his dorsal mane by the withers and swing my right leg over the beast and wrap my thighs tightly on either side. I barely settle myself on his back before the rapid descent begins.

Once underwater, the harpies spread their wings wide, using them as fins to follow me. I hang on tight as I make my literal, and figurative downward spiral.

Above me, the waters are calm, no longer threatening to sink the ship. The jellyfish stop their climbing efforts and the fish stop leaping. Even the seagulls dissipate.

If there's one thing I can always guarantee, it's that the chaos will follow me.

TWELVE

Along the way, many creatures choose to swim beside me. Some are magical, like the trio of maiden mermaids curiously trailing behind me. Others are of the mortal realm, like the fever of manta-rays soaring through the currents before me.

Regardless of their species, these followers tag along on the journey until the first spike which juts into the sea comes into view. Suddenly, they do not seem keen on following anymore. The manta-rays flutter off, quickly followed by the mermaids. Hel even the hippocampi decide this is a good place to station themselves.

The harpies drift to the waters up above. Stretching out their wings to shake off the excess water, they take flight, returning to their nesting trees that line the eastern coast of the Seven Spike mainland.

If only syrens had not lost their wings, then I might be able to flea with them. But no, my destination was a place none of these voyagers would dare enter uninvited.

Between the fifth and sixth spikes of the Queendom, lies a secluded sea cave, barely visible in the murky waters. A trained eye and a certain level of stupidity is necessary to enter.

When Poseidon first crafted his original syrens to guard the sea whilst he was in Olympus, they chose this island to be their home, their Queendom. They summoned the creatures of the sea to aid them in their vision.

The entrance tunnel was burrowed by a pod of narwhals, who relentlessly dug their way into the back of the sea cave. Crabs came in their droves to collect the debris and keep the tunnel clear as work took place. And glowing coral settled at the end of the tunnel, naturally lighting up the way, and brightening the view before me. Their soft pulsating light illuminates the Clam Gates.

As I enter the entrance, a blaze of bright red hair swims towards me.

"Rhea?" I ask as I swim closer to her, "Why are you on guarding duty?"

Defending the Clam Gates was an honourable task of course, but normally it was a duty only reserved for the injured or pregnant who could not practise singing.

I normally glance away awkwardly when girls bow before me, but for once my eyes are locked on her. The way she subtly supports her stomach and puffs as she straightens herself upright.

Huh. Well, I guess I'll rule out injured then.

"Welcome back, Princess," she says, stepping aside to let me through without questioning me.

"Thanks," I reply, "I didn't know you'd completed your Luring. When is she due to arrive?"

A coy smile pulls at Rhea's lip, "She's set to have the same birthday as you, Princess."

"That's..." I trial off as dread floods through me, as I stare at her belly. The crimson scales and kelp of her tail-skirt are stretched to its limit over her bump. Her rather hefty bump which acts like sand-timer for my own Luring Lullaby; forever looming closer, "...wonderful. Truly wonderful for you. I cannot wait to have a little friend to share the day with."

With that, she lightly bows and returning to her guarding duty. I don't have the heart to tell her the biggest threat to our seas and species lies *within* the damn Queendom.

As I make my way into the main fortress, I notice the deafening silence. There is no welcome wagon. No excited children to wave at the boats, no women waiting to kiss their returning sailors. There is just a long anemone red carpet leading to the coral throne, upon which she sits.

The Queen of the Seven Spikes. My mother.

I opt not to bow, and she opts not to bother with pleasantries. She skips straight to the point.

"You look horrendous," she says flatly, "Your weeks outside the magical realm has aged you significantly, my child. Across your cheeks and by your eyes, the skin, it's uneven, it folds almost..."

Her somewhat ethereal voice takes me back. I forgot what she sounds like when she's not in my mind or controlling a hippocampus.

"They're lines from this human emotion called *laughter*. You should try it sometime," I retort.

"It's unfortunate to see your attitude has not improved," she cuts, her tail flicks with frustration, "You have much to learn. Luckily we have all the time in the universe."

She purposely emphasises *all the time* just to see me shudder. She looks blissfully delighted when I almost gag, simply reclining further into her throne, "I guess it should come as no surprised your disgusting temper has worsened. Wasting your time and immortality with a son of Ares is bound to have that effect."

I bite my tongue but swallow harder than normal. It's subtle, but she notices.

"Did you think I wouldn't know what was going on in my seas?" she asks, relishing in my surprise.

"Poseidon owns the seas, not you. Do not reach above your post, mother," I spit.

"If anyone is reaching above their post it is you, Wren. Acting as if you are greater than you are, stronger than you are. You could not even mentally block the cries of a hippocampus."

She cackles an ugly laugh without any humour, "As if it weren't embarrassing enough you allowed yourself to get caught in a fishing net like a common cod-"

"*Allowed* myself?" I ask hysterically, "Does no-one care about the *net* part of what happened?"

"You did not fight as much as you could have, you know it to be true. If you did you would've died trying, yet here you swim. Not only did you get caught by a net, but you disgraced yourself by allowing some warlord to place a permanent hold on you. You naively traded one trap for another."

Of course, she knows about the binding spell. If she can get inside my head, she can most certainly feel the change in my ichor. The magical itch that scratches at my veins, demanding to be dealt with. I slap the inside of my elbow as if to batten the irritation away. Gods above, don't I have enough to deal with right now?

My mother watches me with a scrutinizing eye that could almost be confused with a look of concern, "I will not lose my only heir to a broken binding oath."

"Let me go then," I offer with no sarcasm. I suggest it as a genuine plea, "I have no desire to be here, and it's not as if you love me."

I hate the mildly optimistic and questioning tone that slips into my voice. I have given up on a Princess-Queen relationship, but apparently some sliver of me I cannot banish which still holds hope she could be my mother. Maybe she could still care about *me*, regardless of me being next in line.

She pushes herself off the throne and drifts slowly towards me. With her gold, woven crown and lengthy crimson tail, she looks every bit regal. She reaches out her long, slim arms and I fear she may hug me. She does not.

"For once you're right. I do not love you."

With the simple flick of her wrist, mermen guards swim towards me, encompassing me from all sides.

I wish I could pretend this is just anger, that she is simply disappointed with me, but alas a syren life is one of brutal honesty.

"I will find this war-bloodied princeling and drag him to our world. I don't care if I must sink every ship in the sea or flood every forsaken island that brat has claimed, he will learn that nothing is ever taken from me lightly. You will finally commit yourself to this Queendom. Show your strength and potential to the rest of the syrens and the magical realm."

"No," I shout and lurch forward. But a dozen hands already have me in their hold.

"You will take his life, and together we will take his lands. Seven Spikes is becoming overcrowded and we shall use his islands...."

She continues to scheme but I no longer hear her threats. Spots cloud my vision and a ringing sound muffles everything in my ears.

The omen is creeping ever closer and I do not know how to stop it. I don't even know if I can.

Had the Weavers of Fate already woven this path, or was there a way I can plead with them to unravel their work?

THIRTEEN

Like everything else in this stagnant world, my chambers have not changed in the slightest since I left. The familiarity of my room is not comforting; it's stifling. I'm not the same girl who once resided here, and the faraway memories of her life smother me. The usual itch in my legs to run sparks once again.

Glancing at my legs, I realise the itch sensation could also be from the mortal pants clinging to my frame in its sodden state. Everyone else is in their finned form besides me, and although I consider remaining barelegged just to be stubborn, the weight of walking through water is exhausting. Instead, I open my coral closet and select my favourite indigo tail-skirted dress. I smooth the hem, pushing out any air bubbles. The fabric lies flush against me, feeling like a second skin.

Without even trying my magic slowly begins to drip feed into the skirt. Once it fuses to my body, it becomes a part of me, forming the much-needed tail for sub-aqua life.

A knocking call is sung outside my chambers and although I cannot see her, I would recognise that delicate voice anywhere.

Dove rounds the corner, beaming her wide smile, "I heard a certain prodigal Princess has returned."

I dive across the room, leaving a stream of bubbles in my wake, "You have no idea how much I have missed you."

She reaches out her arms and I immediately swim into her hug. No amount of time can erase this muscle memory. The feeling of how we just fit into each other's hold. The old gods have a concept of soulmates, and although I do not fully understand the idea, I swear she is mine.

"Wow, those humans have rubbed off on you. Are you crying?"

Her laugh makes me cry even more as she gently prises me from her hold. She pushes a mound of hair out of my face, but it drifts back again.

"Even your hair is rebellious. Sit over here and let me fix this mop."

Having never seen the mortal realm, she has endless questions for me. I answer as best as I can, sparing no details about how mesmerizing flames and candles are, how acidic pickles taste most importantly how frustrating men are.

"Do you remember the bereaved King who called for his family across the seas? Well, I met his son, and he's equally as...passionate."

"How could I forget? You went out nightly for weeks because you were afraid your mother would drown his rowboat. Gods, you were only a child at the time," she smiles, before her face sours a little, "I mean, of course, we *all* were children."

Sailors once coined the nickname "*The Cicadas of the Sea*," for syrens, because we don't have staggered age groups like mortals. Every seventeen to eighteens new syrens are born like a plague. No one remembers how this tradition started, but the Queen suggests it maximises are harmonies within the choir and promotes loyalty as children are reared all together. The only person who can birth children outside of luring years is the Queen.

"Did you ever think about why your mother never lured King Lachlan? She's opportunistic by nature, and he was an easy target," Dove asks, obviously following my trail of thought. She eases her braiding, but continues with her questions, "Did you ever find it odd she didn't have another heir? No offence Wren, but with you being such a flight risk, why wouldn't she produce another daughter for security? Throughout the Queendom history, most monarchs have had at least four or five daughters. Hel, Queen Swan of the seventh generation had eleven daughters!"

"I don't know, Dove. Why don't you ask her instead?" I sass, "And where did you learn about Queen Swan?"

All history slates were shattered under my mothers rule. She insisted we could only move forward if we didn't waste time looking back.

"When you swam-away I was intensely interrogated as to your whereabouts. Thankfully you leaving without telling me meant I couldn't tell them anything, because I honestly didn't know. So instead, I was eel-shackled within the whale-rib hold"

An invisible anchor pulls down my heart, "You were placed in the whale-ribs? Dove, I'm so sorry, I...I.."

I cannot bring myself to finish my sentence, as no apology would ever be good enough. She was shunned to a holding cell at the very perimeter of the Queendom. Trapped inside a skeleton prison who those who have lost their minds, normally reserved for syrens whose minds had been scrambled by the frequencies of singing. But because of my actions, my best friend had landed in there.

She brushes away my tears and apology with a flick of a finger, "Shh, I don't have time for tears. I need you to listen. I don't think those sent to the skeleton are as crazy as they're made out to be. Those *deranged and rambling* syrens were not hearing fragmented tunes and song echoes in their minds. They were hearing hindsight and omens."

I stiffen instantly at the word, "What do you mean *omens?*"

"They are hundreds of tiny drawings carved into the bones surrounding me. I couldn't decode all of them, but one series of symbols repeated more than others. A beakless bird handing over its wings to a god in exchange for power," she says, with an awaiting expression.

Having no idea what she's getting at, I just shrug and worry perhaps she has gone mad. Maybe the insanity of the past prisoner's lurked in the water and soaked through her skin.

"Well, have you ever heard the Queen sing?" she asks with a keen eyebrow.

"I mean, of cour-" I splutter, my voice catching in my throat unable to say the words as they are a lie.

I rack my brain for memories of her singing, but I come up short. Granted, her tormenting voice was always in my mind, but never her tune, come to think of it, "No, I haven't heard her sing myself. But seeing as she has a daughter, then she would have performed the Luring Lullaby like everyone else."

Feeling more and more confined, I move away from her and begin to pace, swimming the length of my chamber.

"The Queen has never performed a luring because she has no singing voice, Wren. She's the beakless bird depicted!"

"Dove..." I start, not knowing where to start at all, "This is crazy, you don't honestly believe-

"She's the mute bird who sacrificed our wings to Poseidon as part of a deal. He accepted the offering, using our feathers to craft Pegasus. In return, she wanted power. Yet Poseidon knew she would be a tyrant with a song-voice, and she most certainly couldn't be handed raw power. Instead, Poseidon gave her the only blessing she would never be able to obtain herself. Not having a voice means no luring, ergo no daughters. So..." Dove rambles to herself, before sighing and looking at me with a seriousness I'm not used to, "Poseidon gave her you."

I abruptly stop swimming. The gentle current against my side threatens to knock me off my tailfins as I struggle to stay upright. Dove is off rambling again, but I cannot hear her words over the blood rushing through my ears. I squeeze my eyes shut, hoping to wake up when I open them but no such luck. This isn't another nightmare. This is real.

"...And that's why she is consumed with her need to control you. She sacrificed so much in her attempt for more power, yet the gods gave her you. It's no wonder she sees you as a damn power vault and not her daughter. You are the voice she never had."

"Why the Hel are you telling me this?" I exclaim. A torrent of bubbles escapes from my gills. They float upwards undisturbed, only to burst against the sharp shard of the stalactites.

"Because the time has come, Wren. With no history to look back on, the Queen's toxic beliefs have become our new traditions. Syrens were created to be guardians of the sea, to *help* sailors find their way. We were never meant to be confined behind the Clam Gates! None of us have even seen the island of Seven Spikes because we're afraid we'll decay somehow if we swim past those gates, and-"

"Stop," I snap, momentarily leaning against the rough rock behind me. I shake my head wildly, threatening to undo Dove's handiwork, "Just stop it, okay? This is too much. What am I meant to do with this *speculation?*"

"Wren," Dove says softly, taking both my hands, "I promise you this is the truth."

The magic which binds us to honesty ripples in the air between us. She offers me a sympathy wince, "Even if I could somehow lie, I would never ever lie to you, and especially not about this. When your mother bartered our wings away for her own selfish desires, the gods knew she was an unfit ruler. So, they gave her the power she desired in the form of an heir. A daughter who would be stronger and more righteous than her. She was gifted her own demise."

I sink onto my knees, and thankfully she remains quiet for a few moments. The silence does nothing to add my reeling mind. The waves of thoughts and questions crash around inside my head, but one rises higher than the rest.

"What am I meant to do?" I manage to whisper over the storm of chaos in my mind.

Dove kneels beside me, "The carving did not predict an outcome, but I think visiting your creators would be a good place to start."

The gods are said to reside in the Eastern Acropolis, an ancient citadel located in the centre of Saturn Reef. Only those with a heart of steel would dare navigate those dense rings of the reef protecting the mountainous isle. On the highest peak lies a pantheon, guiled from gold and ichor.

"No one has ever successfully reached Saturn Reef. Or if they have, they never made it back to talk about it," I sigh, hanging my head in my hands, "It's so far east it's almost bloody west!"

"It's a long voyage, there's no denying it. I don't mean to rush you, but you should leave soon. You need to get as far a head start as you can before the Queen notices you're gone," Dove explains, making her way over to my bed, and lying down.

I open my mouth to make a snarky comment about how now is not the ideal naptime, when I feel a pull in my core.

Magic ripples through the room as Dove whispers "*o kathréftis mou.*" It's a chant I have not heard since we were mischievous children, switching places for choir practice. *My mirror.*

I blink twice, not believing the transformation before my eyes. Dove's hair darkens to my navy hue, and her skin becomes peppered with subtle scars from years of misadventure.

Sensing my resistance, she purposely uses a chirpy tone, it's her oldest trick in the book.

"C'mon it'll be like old times when I used to huddle in your bed whilst you watched over King Lachlan. Besides time moves differently here, there's a chance you'll be back before she even notices!"

She says it with a smile. But it's not her smile, it's mine. It's a pained grimace.

With everything suddenly feeling too fast-paced in this slow water world, I turn away no longer able to look at her.

"Say the words," she coaxes from behind me.

"My most caring and gallant *adelfi*," I whisper, my voice cracking as I blurt out the old word for *sister*.

I begrudgingly clear my throat and repeat her words, allowing magic to morph my appearance as well.

I always knew she was more selfless than me, but I never thought I'd be such a coward that I couldn't look her in the eye to say good-bye.

Without wasting another second, I swim slowly towards the door my chambers but catch a glimpse of my reflection in the mirror.

It might be the most beautiful I've ever looked, but it's the ugliest I've ever felt.

FOURTEEN

As I approach the Clam Gates, Rhea moves away from the ledge along the wall and offers a wide, friendly smile. Her warmth perplexes for me a moment until I remember her and Dove are chamber-mates and both sopranos.

"You're not heading out, are you?" Rhea askes, with a confused brow, "I wasn't told anyone would be leaving tonight."

I smile back with as much Dove essence as I can, whilst my Wren mind panics behind the facade. I cannot lie to her, what am I meant to say. Think, damnit, think.

The dim light from the glowing coral glints off black shells in the distance, sparking an idea.

"Well, Wren loves mussels," I say truthfully, gesturing towards the shellfish in the distance.

"Oh, sure," Rhea nods, moving aside to let me through, "The Princess deserves anything she wants after returning. I'm sure she got quite the earful from her mother."

"Yeah she sure did," I laugh lightly, as I swim through the gate.

"I hope she comes to reign soon," Rhea says quietly, resting her hand across her swollen belly.

"Me too," I admit to her and myself as I swim towards the rocks housing the mussels.

Once Rhea is back on her ledge, I drop the shells, letting them drift to the bottom of the seafloor, and I dive out of view.

Feeling numb from the inside out, I don't have the energy to swim upwards. Instead, I gradually float to the surface until I'm bobbing on my back. As my magic dissolves, so does my faux Dove resemblance. Granted her appearance was a mere ruse but letting go of it is like abruptly stepping out of a hug. All too soon I'm alone and back to being me, a combination which does my frazzled mind no good.

Staring blankly at the night skies overhead, I begin to map out familiar constellations above me. I hope to remind myself although my life feels like it is crumbling apart, the larger world still exists, it still relentlessly spins on.

With a pointed finger, I trace a path from the horns of Taurus, to strings of the Lyra, glance at the glowing moon, and end the trail with the tip of Pegasus' tail, the brightest star above me. As I hoped, it brings a sense of stillness and belonging.

I take a few deep breaths before I'm suddenly caught for air. I look at the moon once more.

The last remnant of a waxing crescent moon barely shines above me. But it had just been a full moon when I attacked the island.

How long had I been underwater?

Calculating lunar phases in my racing mind, I guess I must have been down below for about seven or eight days.

Of course, I knew time moves slower in the water world. It was a key factor in my wanting to leave, but I'm unsure if I will ever get used to how fast things move in the mortal world.

I lost a whole week. Shit.

I try to remain calm. I try to convince myself the tightening sensation in my chest is my fault, it's just my own panic. I try and try but lying has never been my speciality.

As my body realises how long I've been away from Kellan, the ichor in my blood begins to sprint. It races through my veins as it searches for him.

You have my oath that I will return to you, King Kellan, is the only discernible sentence I hear through the ringing in my ears. The rest is just a muffle of dread.

I fling my arms wide, an invitation to nearby rays, hippocampi, even a damn jellyfish to aid my journey. Yet nothing comes. I lower my lips to the water and summon enough breath to release a calling song. But no creature answers my tune.

Of course not. They're all in service to the Queen, not her abdicating heir. They will only aid me if it's a direct order or somehow benefits their ruler.

Although I still don't know what it means I repeat the ancient curse I once heard Kellan say.

I like the way it feels in my mouth, so I yell it to the night sky. It fuels my adrenaline and somewhat calms my nerves. With no other option, I turn my back to the East, blocking out all thoughts of Saturn Reef from my mind.

Instead, I use the constellations above me to orientate myself south. Once I'm lined up for Lunar Lands, I start swimming and I don't stop.

For the next two days, I try everything and anything to make the journey easier. I paddle near the surface.

I drift along the currents.

I dive deep down.

I do anything to swim constantly, to keep moving, yet the voyage feels endless. The relentless pull inside my chest demands me to move forward as if Kellan himself were reeling me in. I'm pretty sure even if I die, my corpse will still float its way towards him.

It is on the third morning I'm convinced I *am* a corpse. I must have died at some stage during the night, my soul snuck away with the tide because there is no way I could be alive and feel this numb.

My arms can no longer break the waters before me. Stiffened and bruised, they lay lifeless at my side. My muscles have been replaced with worn, frayed ropes. Mere threads keep my limbs intact with my body.

Long gone are my once-powerful and precise kicks, instead, my feet *pat* the waves below, a repetitive action I doubt I'll ever be able to stop.

Feeling like sodden driftwood, I am forced to let the breaking waves toss and turn me.

Seafoam slaps and sticks to my face. With its airy white bubbles and fluffy texture, it resembles the delicate loaves of bread I feasted on in the cottage.

Sticking out my sandpaper dry tongue, I lick the foam only to dissolve the bubbles and be left with salt on my lips.

A small voice in the back of my head tries to say something but I cannot make sense of it. I think it's my voice, although I no longer remember what I sound like. Come to think of it, I can no longer recall my name.

The survival part of me gets pissed off with my lolling about. The small voice shouts louder. Seafoam. Why can I see, and *lick* seafoam?

The waters are getting shallower. With an enormous amount of effort, I lift my chin just enough to gaze upon the horizon. I blink away the seawater and focus on the rock formation before me.

Once my hazy eyes recognise the view, they immediately well with hot tears. A sob catches in my throat.

Before me stands the sea stacks. The gateway pillars between the Meteoroid Spit and Crescent Cove.

I *actually* did it.

I was almost there.

Maybe Dove was right, maybe I could do this.

With the full power of the sea being channelled into a current surrounding me, I'm quickly driven forward by the rapids. I'm soaring through the water without effort. I should be able to drift my entire way into the bay! Then the pounding in my chest, the gushing in my ears and everything else will finally ease once I see him.

Kellan.

The man whose face has been constantly tormenting me the past few days. Most of me hates him for this binding oath. I want to punch him in his stupid chiselled jaw for the unbearable pain he is causing me. I warned him, the damn righteous fool, that this would happen. It seems he would rather kill me than lose me.

But a smaller part of me, a sliver I have tried and failed to banish over the past few days, lusts for him.

The same delirious part of my mind confusing seafoam for bread wants nothing more than to fall into his strong arms. For him to take away the burning pain in my veins, soothe the ache in my chest and remind me of my name.

He has placed this wretched curse on me, but he is also the enticing cure.

A vague memory of his serious face on bated breath as we made our way through the sea stacks flashes behind my frazzled mind. Why the Hel had he been worried? This current is amazing! Yet he hadn't relaxed until the banners were raised.

Although to be honest, he always has a brooding expression. Not allowing my mind to get distracted yet again with another montage of Kellan memories, I brush it off as him being his temperamental self. But I fail.

As if the sea heard my inner dialogue it reminds me why. The jagged rocks of a dozen smaller sea stacks lying just below the surface.

The rapid I was enjoying a mere twenty seconds ago has now become the Styx. The river of death determined to deliver me to Hades himself.

With my body too exhausted to swim out of the current, I'm tossed and thrown in the turbulent waters. My body slams into a hidden stack. My left-hand side takes most of the blunt force, with my forearm splitting open against the shale. The slice happens so fast and silently, I almost don't notice. The pummelling waters mask the pain in with the rest of my beatings. My inky blue ichor easily merges into the murky waters surrounding me. I could nearly pretend it didn't happen if it weren't for the major inconvenience it has brought.

The wound acts like an open dam, allowing my ichor to finally escape. The magic in my veins is bound to the King who's on the *other* side of this cove. My ichor does not just seep out with my blood, it rushes. It runs frantically and instinctively towards him. My body begins to feel lighter as I slip away. The riptide flips me over onto my back once more.

There is no moon above me.

No constellation to guide me. Nothing but the cool winter sun holding no heat. Its glare burns my sobbing eyes. I go to look away when I see something move above me.

On the edge of the sea stack is Ludwig. He stares at me, his gaping mouth as wide as his scared eyes. He shrieks and sprints off in the opposite direction.

Seeing an inky trail emerging from a half-dead syren? I don't blame him for running away. He should feel fear. I should have too. I close my heavy eyes from the bright skies above and everything goes black.

I assumed death would ease the pounding in my chest, but even in death, I'm wrong apparently. The repetitive thumping against my ribs ruins any momentary peace I had. The world around me is still black, but it's as if someone is knocking on a door somewhere.

I ignore it, wandering deeper into the void.

Thump.

Thump.

Thump.

Gods above, what does a syren have to do to die in peace around here! The spike of aggravation forces me to pause my descend into death. I spin in my heel and mentally march around the void of my mind. How do I stop this damn thudding so I can finally sleep?

I fling my eyes open to see Fletcher hovering over me, pounding on my ribcage.

Twisting at the hips, I upheave a lungful of saltwater and a bellyful of bile onto the dock beneath me. It fuses with my ichor, which still gushes from my arm.

Fletcher has stopped pounding my heart back into a functioning state, but his wide eyes are willing me to stay alive.

I open my mouth, but no air goes in and no words come out. I forgot about my gills which still have not retracted. Was anything going to go my way today?

Nessa comes into view and swiftly drops to her knees. Her trembling hand reaches out to touch the stained dock. Her fingertips come away tainted with the various colours of my being.

"Oh shit," she exclaims. Who knew such a perfectly poised mouth could make such sounds?

Fletcher keeps his jewelled hands squeezing a lethal grip around my gaping forearm as if to hold it together.

"Fetch the healer," Fletcher shouts towards Nessa. The panic is thick in his voice, and I wish there was a way I could tell him not to worry. There's no point. I won't make it.

"And the King!" he adds.

Though I know her efforts will be futile, I appreciate the way Nessa takes off. Her arms and long legs pumping as she crosses the town square. She vanishes around a corner, and I vanish into the darkness once more.

FIFTEEN

Someone shakes me roughly. Even with my eyes closed, it's clear who this persistent nuisance is. The man who hates to lose is not willing to let me go. Of course, he arrived before the healer, everything is a competition to him.

Oath.

I repeat it in my head over and over until I somehow stumble the word out loud.

Without hesitation, Kellan hauls me upright, wrapping a strong arm around me. My head flops against his solid chest in an unnatural fashion, suddenly feeling far too heavy for my neck to support.

He thumbs my chin and places his forehead against mine, "I release you from your oath, Wren. You kept your word. You returned to me."

Wren! That was it. How did I ever forget my name?

As the binding oath retracts, something inside of me eases, yet it brings no release. Perhaps the fury in my fight was the only thing keeping me alive.

My gills flap like a heartbeat. How in the Underworld do I still have gills? Surely, it's been hours, if not days, by now...not mere minutes.

Rhymical and steady they throb until they begin to slow down. But then everything else begins to slow down too.

I thought the breakneck speed in which I transitioned before would kill me, but this, this is somehow worse. The world around me gradually dwindles, and it becomes obvious I won't survive this. I'll simply slip through the cracks and somewhere between my land and sea form, I will cease to exist.

Somewhere between me and him, I will be lost. No longer a syren, or an heir. Nor a weapon, or a monster. I'll also lose any chance I had of becoming the person I so badly wanted to be.

Kellan somehow pulls me a fraction closer. I can no longer tell where he ends nor where I begin.

His usual scent gently fills my nose. It's the first non-sea related scent I've inhaled in a fortnight. It's more glorious than I remember.

He lightly thumbs the vanishing line in my skin as my gill slits fully disappear.

I'm vaguely aware of my body being tilted forward. A sharp tip presses through my dress at my shoulder. The sensation is swiftly followed by a loud *rip*, as the fabric covering my left arm is slashed away.

"What are you doing?" Callum's voice wheezes as if he's just run the length of the island.

There's a growing background hum as a crowd begins to gather. Fletcher uses his Master of the Sails tone to try to keep people from constricting the already claustrophobic circle, ordering citizens to give me space and move away from the King.

Kellan's voice rumbles through his chest and reverberates against my skin, "She's losing too much, she won't live without it."

"Kellan, it might not even work-"

"But it might, and I'll take those odds," he cuts off Callum with a clipped tone, "You can either help or leave, brother."

Wordlessly, a second pair of hands hold me steady, although they are not needed. I can no longer move, so there's no fear of me going anywhere...except maybe to Hades.

"Do you remember the words?"

"As if I could ever forget," Kellan says.

There's another ripping sound, yet I feel no fabric loosen. Instead, my arm is met with a stinging sensation that spreads to the rest of my body. Sticky, warm, mortal blood steeps into my system.

No, not mortal blood. Descendants blood laced with ichor.

"Kellan," I croak but he does not hear me. I barely hear myself over his raspy chanting.

He calls on the gods using their archaic, mostly forgotten prayers. The consecrated chant is mainly gibberish to my ringing ears, but a single word resonates within my core.

Meraki.

The ancient concept of pouring a piece of your soul into something you cherish.

He smears an old symbol onto my arm, over and over until I feel the movement even without him touching me.

I feel clammy against his heat, yet I do not move away.

Maybe it's because I am too weak. Maybe it's because I don't want to.

I guess there are worse places to die. The babble of the town fades away until I hear nothing but Kellan.

Meraki.

Meraki.

Meraki.

My body shudders once, then I go limp in his hold.

SIXTEEN

I wake up.

Which by itself would be shocking enough. But to awake in the same room as Kellan is a level of jolting I cannot handle right now.

He's asleep in a wicker chair across the room. A room in which I have never seen before but assume is the King suite.

Thick sheepskin rugs line the cobbled floors, heavy curtains line ample windows giving views of the whole island. Judging by the stiff set creases I doubt the drapes were ever drawn shut. Kellan does have a love of light in any form so it would make sense.

Starlight and a gentle glow from the town lanterns floods through the window. My eyes follow the illuminated slanted square that spills across the bed, covers the rugs, and casts a soft glow on the set of wicker chairs positioned near a wide-mouthed fireplace.

The two chairs look like they're silently straining to hold Kellan, as he spills his muscular weight between them. His long leg stretched onto the other chair, boots still on, and his bent elbow rests against the arm of the chair which props his head at an awkward angle. If he were to be wearing a crown it would fall. Although come to think of it, I have yet to see him wear one.

In his resting state, he doesn't look like a King. He isn't wearing his official jacket or epaulettes anymore. He dons his heavy open cloak over a scruffy loose knit jumper. In here without his admiring people, ceremonial robes, or forceful fleet behind him, he's just Kellan.

Granted he's less intimidating than his normal regal self, but something about him keeps me on edge.

Behind him is a smouldering fire almost lifeless bar a few embers as stubborn as him. Over the back of the chair holding his heavy boots, lies my tail skirt. Thin wisps of steam dispatch. The smell of hot, damp fabric fills the air between us.

Looking at myself, it dawns on me I'm wearing yet another one of Kellan's cloaks. Did he put this on me?

I untuck my hair to cover my blushing cheeks and instead tuck my knees, pulling them close to my chest. My legs are completely free, as are my wrists. No part of me is tethered and I can't even see my syren bridle in the dimly lit room. The only metal object in my view is Kellan's blade which rests atop the mantelpiece.

Gods above, he isn't even armed in my company. Maybe I should attack him just for a sense of normality....

I swing my legs free from the blankets and set them on the floor. My shuffling wakes him from his light slumber and stops me moving any further. He opens a single, blearily eye, smacks his lips and takes one look at me.

"Look who's alive," he says in a hoarse voice, a tired smile pulling at his lips.

My heart lurches. I hate it. At least I think I do.

He remains in his sprawled-out position but runs a hand through his messy hair. His stained sleeve slips, revealing a raw, barely sealed knife wound the length of his forearm that will most definitely scar.

I glance at my arm to see it's still somehow attached. Oh gods, the chant!

"Are you alright?" My voice drips with poorly hidden concern which he notices immediately.

"Ah, it takes more than a papercut to kill a young warlord," he says with his usual finesse. But he sounds exhausted and looks even paler than usual.

I try to convince myself it's just the low light of the room playing tricks on me. It can't be my fault. I can't deal with the guilt right now, even if he is a pain in the ass.

"Wren?" he calls, even though I'm the only person in the room. My attention is already fully on him.

"Never leave me again."

"I didn't exactly *leave*, the sea-"

"I don't care if the sea bursts through the window with a handwritten invitation for you, you do not leave. Do you understand?"

"Are you asking for another binding oath?" I grate out with as much sass as I can muster.

"No, I'm promising you that anywhere you go, I will follow. Nothing will take you from me."

The heavy tone of possession in his voice pulls in my core. I expect his words to feel like a threat or even a curse, but they do not. Instead, I find solace in them. Maybe he's so stubborn and righteous he could best my mother. Maybe it's his ichor flowing through my veins, or the fact I know how much he hates to lose, but I fully believe him.

"You could not have followed where I went. You cannot survive beneath the waves."

"Then you'll never go there again. I meant what I said, Wren. Together, or not at all."

Together, or not at all.

He might be Hel bent on never losing me to my mother again, but she will come for me. And together or not, she will not be defeated.

"I need to rest a while longer. We both do," he says, shuffling his weight in his seat, "So sleep, and still be here when I awake. We need to talk. No more half-truths."

The urge to run away tingles in my legs, but I tuck them under the still warm blanket hoping the fabric can weigh them down. I'm growing weary of never staying in one place for very long, and I guess there are worse places to be.

He drifts back to sleep almost immediately, which leaves me lying there, listening to his light snores.

SEVENTEEN

At some stage during the night, Kellan relocates to the empty space beside me. He mumbles something about being too hot, or too cold, or maybe ending up with the posture of Cyclops? I wasn't really listening, and he rambled a lot before quickly falling back asleep.

I thought having him so near would bother me more than it does. Although if he ever asked, I would kick up a colossal stink and deny how it's the most soothing sleep I have had in months, if not years.

For once, I wake without terror chasing me to the surface. There is no sweat, no splinters from broken tables. Just a gentle knocking on the door.

Kellan groans face down into his pillow before grunting, "Come in."

A thousand thoughts dash through my half-asleep mind. Should I bolt and stand by the dresser? Should I stay where I am and act like Kellan being so close is not a talking point? Maybe I should just pretend to be asleep....

Before I commit to any action, Callum opens the door to find me half in, half out of the bed, looking fully guilty. I reason with myself I have nothing to feel uncomfortable about, but it does little to stop my cheeks blushing as Callum's eyes spot my bare legs hanging out the side of his brothers' bed.

I reel my leg back to the safety of the blanket as if it were a hooked fish and Callum physically shakes off whatever question he's tempted to ask. Instead, he crosses the room with a heavy footstep to stand at the bedside.

"Are you still alive?" he asks, prodding Kellan's shoulder with two fingers.

"I beckoned you in, didn't I?" Kellan muffles into his pillow.

Callum ignores the quip and instead lifts Kellan's left arm for inspection. The wound no longer bleeds but it's raw and appears puffy with swelling.

Pulling a familiar brooding face that I've seen more than enough of in the past few weeks, Callum sighs and lowers the arm, "It's too early to know for sure, but I fear infection."

"I'm fine," Kellan says firmly. But he does not sound fine, and he most certainly doesn't look it.

"He was complaining of feeling too hot during the night, I believe that is a symptom, right?" I pose my question direct to Callum which causes Kellan to grumble.

He rolls onto his side to face me. Golden locks tumble out of place to frame his face.

"Careful Wren, it almost sounds like you're worried about me." He flashes his wolfish smile, but it falls short of reaching his eyes. It seems even that would take too much energy.

Feeling entirely too close to him, but not wanting to repeat the awkwardness of trying to vacate the bed, I busy myself with examining my wound. Even with my eyes scouring over my forearm, I feel his gaze on me.

The laceration I received is more jagged as it was inflicted from a rock and not a blade, but it is not as long or tender looking as his. There is minimal risk of infection, yet I'm coming down with something much worse.

Empathy. Their stupid mortal conditions are rubbing off on me.

"A heightened temperature is a definite sign," Callum says pointedly. He slaps an analysing, flat palm across his brother's forehead with more force than necessary, "Good observation, Wren."

"I can patch a poultice to draw out infection. It should be easy to find fresh moss and seaweed strips on the island. I'll fuse some of my magic into it," I suggest.

Callum nods vigorously, "That would be helpful. There's a healer on Meteoroid Spit who tends to the sailors, but ichor wounds are above mortal abilities. I'll have some sent to the suite, along with food."

Kellan sits upwards. He tries to conceal the effort it takes, but the fleeting wince across his face is not missed by Callum or me.

"Will you both stop? I told you I'm fine. And I'll get my own bloody food-"

"You performed the Chant of Life, Kellan," Callum cuts him off, "The first time the citizens of these isles heard that was when Dad tried to save Mom after Aveen was born. They heard it again when you tried to revive Dad. No one needs reminding on how those events turned out. The people have not forgotten."

148

A dream-like memory of Callum asking Kellan if he remembered the words floats into my head. Of course, he knew the chant to say and the symbols to draw. He had tried the ritual with Lachlan but had failed. I don't think it's something you would forget a second of.

The guilty knot in my core constricts even more. So, why had the ritual worked with me?

Kellan winces once more but this time the pain is not caused by his arm. He opens his mouth, but Callum isn't finished.

"And you couldn't get your own *bloody* food because you don't have the strength to get through the crowds of people waiting to see you. Fletcher and I spend the last hour ordering the sailors to do fruitless tasks to stop them sauntering around the harbour hoping to catch a glimpse of you. There was a vigil held overnight led by the townswomen. They used the dripping wax from their prayer candles to veil the ichor and blood-stained dock. The Virginal Temple of Athena is almost inaccessible from the sheer mass of wreaths and flowers being laid on the steps."

"Alright, alright," Kellan snaps with a tone of authority not to be tested, "You've made your point."

The two of them stare at each other. The tension in the room is palpable and suffocating.

Perhaps I could slip out of the bed now? I get the feeling I could be fully naked, yet they would be too busy puffing out their chests to even notice.

"Ares might be in our veins, but you can still die. Dad was tougher than any of us and he died of a measly heart attack. How much more of a mortal ending can you meet? Stop acting like you're so indestructible. You don't wait for back up boats when storming an island, you don't let anyone help, I just..." Callum's face flushes with temper, his mouth stammering to find the words through the haze of his anger.

"I know," Kellan soothes, "I'll try harder to not push help away, okay? I'm sorry Cal."

"Our people need their King. I need my brother, as does Aveen."

The mere mentioning of her name softens the friction between them. Seizing the opportunity to remind them I am in the damn room and hopefully change the subject, I ask "How is she?"

"She's okay. Understandably worried, but she's mostly just upset Kellan couldn't style her hair before her lessons."

"I assumed being held hostage with her would force you to learn how to braid her hair, but no, you're still as futile as ever,"

"Kellan!" I shrill.

Callum immediately fires a pillow at Kellan with a vile curse and a wide smile. The two erupt into laughter.

With my mouth hanging open, I glance from one to the other. How was that insult funny? I don't think I will ever understand brother bonds. Maybe I'll just never understand men in general.

I'm beginning to learn they possess a certain level of insanity you must be raised around to deem normal behaviour.

Callum gives Kellan a firm slap on the back and makes his way towards the door.

"I'll arrange for food, moss and seaweed to the sent to the suite and I'll spread the word you're still alive and just as annoying as ever."

"Wait," I holler just before he closes the door, "Could you arrange for some clothes to be sent too?"

Callum pops his grinning head around the doorframe, "Sure, you wear a size 'Kellan', right?"

I bury my head under the pillow and try to block out the sound of their laughter.

Although it is not humanly possible to sleep anymore, apparently, it's feasible for a syren. I don't realise I have drifted back into a slumber until a small voice appears beside me.

"Are you sure she's not dead? Ludwig seemed pretty sure she was dead?" Aveen asks, peering closer to me.

"No, she is not dead. Just resting," Kellan whispers loudly, urging her to do the same, "Leave her be and come here, *mikros.*"

Little one.

The way he speaks to her makes my heart skip a beat. Or two. Gods above he's meant to be a wicked tyrant whose unhinged and maleficent. That would be easier for me to hate, but this...I don't know what to do with this.

Even though I am wide awake, I keep my breathing rhythmical, my eyes closed. I fear my mere awake presence would ruin the moment. It normally does.

Once I hear her light footsteps receding, I slowly peer one eye open. Kellan is sitting upright in his wicker chair. The fire blares once more, sending crackling sounds and waves of heat into the room. He listens intently to Aveen's news as if he were at a privy council meeting.

"And I have extra lessons all this week to catch up. It's really not fair, it's not my fault I got kidnapped!"

Although Kellan nods intently and agrees with her woes, I spot his dimple struggling to maintain hidden.

"Will Wren have lots to catch up on when she goes home?" Aveen asks.

I don't know who holds their breath more, me or Kellan.

He clears his throat and runs a hand over his jaw, "Would you mind if she stayed here?"

Aveen earnestly shakes her head, sending her raven tresses flying free from whatever sloppy plait Callum managed this morning, "No, I wouldn't mind. She helped save Cal and me. I like her."

"I do too," he soothes.

It's me; I'm *definitely* the person holding their breath more. Another minute of this and my gills might magically pop open.

Aveen wiggles her way into her brothers lap and asks him to do the pretty braid in her hair. He corrects her by explaining it's a very technical and important sailing knot, not a pretty braid, but he happily does it for her anyway.

Eventually, they left the suite and once their receding footsteps had fully vanished, I took my chance to sneak away.

I wandered my way into the city, clutching the loose coin I found in Kellan's cloak pocket. My main priority was to obtain non-pickled food. Bread, cheese, anything not tasting like raw vinegar. Then, with any leftover coin, I would buy spare clothes, seeing as I somehow ended up in the Kings garments every other day. At least that was my plan, but like most of my agendas, it did not turn out that way.

I had barely laid my eyes on the first stall of fresh food when a frail, wrinkled hand reached out from behind me and tapped my elbow. I turned slowly, expecting to see a river Troll or an elf, but no. Instead, a pocket-size old woman with short white curls presents me with a basket.

The hamper heaved with succulent dates, berry jams and more varieties of cured meats than I could count nor name.

She offered it to me with a curtsy and did not meet my eyes. Yet for once, it was not fear she felt in my presence but respect.

"For you," she said, "To help you recover, and a thank you for saving our family."

I paused for a moment, racking my brain to think about who I saved who could be related to her, but then it dawned on me she meant the royal family.

Our family.

There was something so warm and tender about how they viewed their rulers. I would never refer to my Queen as family, and I share her damn blood.

"It's too much," I said, battening down a lump of emotion. I engross myself with examining the hand-painted labels on the jars.

"It's not enough. I had a tartlet in there too, but it started to turn sour. You were gone for quite a while," she said with a worried tone.

I nodded, not trusting my voice to hold steady.

"Well, never mind. At least you're back now," she soothed with a maternal tone. She nestled the basket into my arms, before moving away between the stalls.

"Thank you," I called out.

She paused, and with a wide, wise smile replied, "You are welcome."

I got the impression the *welcome* she said was more an island embrace than accepted gratitude for the basket.

EIGHTEEN

With a sigh, I stare at the hamper.

Hampers.

I had accumulated two more by the time I got to the cottage. The island chandler had gifted me a crate full of candles and waxy soaps, but it was Shelli, the island tailor who gave me the most elaborate gift of all. She had kept a note of my measurements from previous alterations, and used them to create a figure-hugging, deep shaded, gold gown complete with bronze beading across the bodice.

Tacked to the dress was a hand-written note which suggested I wear it tonight to the latest Ball. Kellan did love a good celebration, any occasion with liqueur or a gambling table, but from the lecture he received from his brother, I knew this party was more Callum's idea. A gala to show strength and happiness towards their people.

I hang the dress off the mantlepiece, just below the oil painting of Lachlan and Iseult, and I cannot help but draw similarities between the gown and its muse.

Bronze and gold. The colours Lachlan chose for these islands when he conquered and unified them. Most people think he was inspired by the array of metal weapons needed to seize the islands and the summer sun that shone overhead. But looking at his wife's image captured on canvas, it was easy to see where he got the inspiration from.

I had once deemed Lachlan an overambitious warlord. I thought he was greedy and crazed to land-grab anything within reach. But now I understand the appeal to build an empire for someone with russet eyes and a golden crown of hair.

I cannot allow myself to wear Shelli's creation. To do so would be a clear statement that I am aligning myself with these islands. That I am an ally to these people, but allies protect each other. And my remaining on these isles will bring them nothing but pain.

Turning my back on the gown and the painting, I grab the baskets of soaps and march down the hallway to the bathtub.

I let the hot water run, using its babbling sounds to drown out my mounting fears of my mother conjuring an eel up the drainpipe. Once filled, I step into the steaming waters and submerge myself up to the shoulders.

In concentric circles, I buff my soaked skin with a stiff square of soap. I scour my top layer until I feel new, scrubbing repeatedly as if I were shedding old scales like a Drakon.

Once I've worn away the soap into an oval shape, I feel remarkably lighter. I dry off and glide my way to the plush sofa in the sitting room, settling down for the evening. It is nowhere near as soft or warm as Kellan's bed, but I need to try and get some rest.

Because come the morning I am leaving these islands. I will not be the downfall for these people's lives. I will voyage alone to the Eastern Acropolis and plead with the gods for answers, because if they have a plan it's about time they shared it.

After an hour of tossing and turning, I decide the room is too quiet. I've grown familiar with the light chatter of people near-by, or at least the taunting calls of my mother inside my head. Without either, my mind takes a dangerous trip down imagination lane.

I shuffle off the sofa and pad my way towards the door. Perhaps leaving it ajar to hear the laughter and bustle from the town party will help soothe my solitude.

As I reach out my hand, the brass knob turns without me touching it. The door yawns open.

Golden light from the lit-up town floods the cobblestones beneath my feet, as Kellan's illuminated face steps inside.

"Going somewhere?" he asks.

"I just can't seem to sleep," I shrug and wordlessly move aside.

"It's probably too loud out there," he suggests as he brushes past me.

Actually, it's the complete opposite, I think to myself as I close the door and shut out the light.

The cottage is not in darkness for long, as he begins lighting an oil lantern and pulling out various candles from the basket.

"I heard the chandler took which a shine to you?" he chuckles.

I nearly snap at him, telling him not to burn them all at once. I was going to cherish them, and ignite them slowly, one at a time. But I cannot take them with me. Candles do not burn in my world.

Selecting a long taper stick, I steal a drop of flame from his candle before helping him to light them all.

I might as well have a single night of happiness before my world comes crumbling down.

"Nightcap? It'll help you sleep," he offers, pulling a half-empty bottle of rum from his pocket. He places it on the table, the liquid shining like molten gold in the candlelight.

"Please tell me the other half of this isn't already sloshing in your stomach?"

He laughs, but shakes his head, "I did drink it yes, but not tonight. I had it on my boat whilst I was searching for you."

"Don't you mean *kidnapping* me?" I correct with a pointed finger. I choose to sit in the chair furthest away from him.

"Semantics...But no, I was referring to the time the sea stole you back."

The possession in his words is not lost on me.

He places the candles around the room, before pulling out a chair to join me. He opts for the one directly across from me.

"Wait, you looked for me?" I ask, tucking my feet under my chair and removing my hands from the table. My actions do little to settle the unease he makes me feel. It's as if he got under my skin without me noticing, and no matter what I do I cannot shake him away.

He nods, pours the liquid into the cap of the bottle and slides it towards me, "A few times a day and every night. Fletcher and Callum came with me some evenings, but I mostly sailed alone."

"Why?"

"You helped save my family and aided my takeover of Soleil Island. I knew the binding oath would force you to resurface and I thought you might need help when it did. And you're owed a hefty coin purse too. It's the least I can do."

"I meant why did you sail alone?"

His eyes find mine. There's a glint of something unfamiliar in his gaze.

His silence makes my heart lurch forward. I think it gets wedged between my ribs as it does not beat for a moment.

Stupid heart.

Maybe I should visit the healer on the Meteoroid Spit and figure out what's causing my persistent palpitations.

A slow, wolfish smile pulls at his lips, "Well I had to sail alone, I couldn't trust you to resist drowning half my fleet with your insistent bellow, now could I?"

And just like that, he's back to his usual annoying self. I roll my eyes, part my lips, and throw the liquid down my throat before I've time to change my mind.

Gah.

I slam the cap back on the table with a shuddering face. He takes it from my shivering fingers and refills it.

I fully expect him to polish the rim of the cap with his sleeve, or at least make a face or snide comment about having to drink from the same vessel but he doesn't.

He drinks slower than I did, somehow enjoying the burning sensation and licks a rogue drop from his lower lip.

"Gods above, how do you drink it?"

"I have peculiar tastes, and you're simply concentrating on the taste too much. We'll play a game to distract you."

"You and your damn games."

"My sailors and I normally play Truth or Dare when we drink, but I suppose you're at a crippling disadvantage with the truth aspect, huh?"

I shake my head, "Inquisitions aren't exactly my idea of fun."

He reaches into his pocket and withdraws out a handful of coins. Island money is still baffling to me, but from what I've learnt he holds the average worker's monthly allowance in a single hand. He selects one of the larger coins and slides it across the table to me.

"Flip it. I'll choose either 'Face' or 'Fin', if I am wrong then I'll drink, if I'm right, you drink. Simple."

I scrunch my nose and examine the coin closely. I don't know how, but this game feels rigged in his favour.

"Alright," I say hesitantly, "But if I find out you're cheating I'll summon Cerberus to chew you up and spit you out."

"Can you summon Cerberus?" he asks with an arched brow.

"I haven't had to try...yet," I say with a shrug.

He chuckles. It's a magnificent melody. There is something so wholly mortal about it, and although I wish otherwise, I find myself savouring the sound and remembering it for future use.

It may not be a syren song, but it's something I wish to practice more of.

"I do not cheat; I just don't lose," he informs me.

"You can't *always* win."

I toss the coin high into the air. It gyrates in the candlelight between us, splashing dots of golden light across Kellan's shadowed face. I catch the coin with both hands.

"Watch me," he says casually, "It's fin."

I unclasp my palms slowly as if I were releasing a dragonfly. I feel his smugness before I even see the coin.

He hands me the refilled cap with a grin, "Best of three?"

NINETEEN

After his third consecutive victory, he doesn't hand the cap to me anymore. Instead, he raises it to his lips.

"I'll be chivalrous and take one for the team."

I roll my eyes, but I deeply appreciate the liquor reprieve, "We're not a team."

He slams the cap down with a curse, "Stop denying this, Wren. We could make a good team."

"Trust me, you do not want me on your team. I shouldn't even be on this island."

"I can protect you, but I need to know what, or *who* I am protecting you from."

Here it is.

The damn talk he demanded we have.

My eyes drift to the bottle of rum. Maybe I should drink just to break the tension. It ought to taste less unpleasant than the bile rising in my throat.

I swallow hard, "I can protect myself."

"I'm sure you can, but do not forget what I said. You are my syren. Together, or not at all. And since you're remaining here on my island, amongst my people, my family, then I need to know about any and all possible threats," Kellan runs a hand through his hair before adding, "So, tell me. Who is he?"

"What?" I splutter, a weird half-strangled laugh escapes my lips.

"The bastard who dragged you back to the sea. The one you have nightmares about. I've gathered he is no mortal, but is he a merman? A Descendant like me? Or a full god? I know my ichor is not as potent as yours, or possibly his, but I will find a way to defeat him-"

"Typical for a son of war to assume it must be a male reigning terror in my life."

My mouth spits out the quip, but my mind is somewhere else entirely. He would be willing to take on a full god to protect me. It's an impossible task, a fight he would lose in a heartbeat, but one he's willing to try. I don't know if I admire his strong sense of confidence or if I'm terrified by it.

"A jilted lover? Spiteful father?" he asks.

"You do know I'm a syren, right? Men in any form are not exactly in abundance in my world. Hence why we are expected to drown boats."

He looks frustrated but also slightly relieved, "Alright then, who are you running from?"

I fall silent.

"What, no more witty remarks? If it is not a god, then it is someone I can defeat."

"*No one* can defeat her." My voice rumbles like thunder.

"Watch me," he repeats, though less playfully this time, "Who is *she* then?"

I stare at him. He unwaveringly stares back. I blink first. Shit.

"My mother." I barely speak the words.

"Your mother?" he snorts. His tone instantly pissing me off.

"Be warned, I inherited my temper from her," I snap, pushing my chair back with such force it scrapes loudly off the ground, "She is invincible."

"Nothing is ever invincible."

"You seem to think you are. What happened to '*I don't lose*'?" I mimic in the smuggest sounding Kellan voice I can muster.

He fends off a smile, but a dimple still dances across his cheek, "I pray that's not actually what I sound like."

I ignore him and make my way towards the wide window. My gaze roams upon the sea. It is relatively calm on the surface, but gods only know what is brewing below.

He stands as well, moving closer until he's beside me. Towering over my left-hand side, entirely too close, once again.

Showing no interest in the ocean, he only watches me. A dangerous move for a man who thinks he can best the tides.

He shrugs nonchalantly as if he can't understand what all my fuss is about, "I'll deal with her. I managed to catch you, didn't I?"

"She is not as foolish as me. She rarely leaves home."

"You told me you did not have a home."

"I don't really. '*Home*' was the wrong word."

He sighs, growing more impatient with my ambiguity, "I do not wish to pry answers from you or abuse your truthfulness. But know I always get what I want, one way or another, and I rarely ask twice for it. The sooner you stop skirting around your secrets, the better. You may not be able to lie, but don't think your picking and choosing of the truth has gone unnoticed."

Deciding to take another step away from my mother, my Queendom was easy. I had decided that fate months ago, if not years.

But opting to move closer to Kellan, his Kingdom and everyone in it is terrifying. Especially when I know the rejection I could face once they know they're doomed if I stay. They're already doomed by me just being here.

The mortal world moves faster than the magical realm, but it will always catch up. And much like when I resurfaced with my binding oath, I fear it will break through the waters with anger and vengeance. She will come for me. It's only a matter of time. Time which is forever dripping away.

I bite my lip, and untuck my hair, "I...I need to leave."

Before I have a chance to move an inch, he places a grounding hand on my hip, "Alright then, where are *we* going? And don't do that."

"Don't do what?" I ask, trying my best to ignore his grip of my waist.

I ignore his calloused fingertips rubbing against the soft skin of my lower back.

I ignore the way his thumb threatens to slip beneath the hem of my pants.

I ignore it all. Or at least I tell myself to.

"Don't bite your lip," he rumbles, "It's incredibly distracting. And annoying."

"You're the annoying one."

It's a childish comeback that would sound more natural coming out of Aveen's mouth, "And I hate-"

You.

Except I cannot say it.

A spasmatic cough catches in my throat. A burning sensation rips through my core as if I swallowed a lump of scorching coal. My entire body convulses against him as I fight for air. I pant until I regain enough control to master shallow and staggered breaths.

Is there any hope he didn't notice? Maybe I just swallowed a fly.

Kellan's already tight grip on my waist somehow tightens. He holds me out at armlength with wide eyes demanding an explanation, "Tell me that you hate me."

Alright, so maybe he did notice, and I can't pass it off as a swallowed fly.

I hastily try to practice the words in my mind. *I hate...I* try to mentally add his name, but I cannot.

Hmm. Okay, well I really hate pickles, so maybe if I say that and trick my mind at the last second, then-

"Tell me, Wren," he presses, ruining my practice.

"I...I can't," I say quietly, wiggling in his hold but I don't move an inch.

He holds me firm in his grasp and cranes his neck downward. Placing his forehead against mine, he bridges the gap between us.

"But you've said it before? More than once," he husks, "I kept count."

His warm lips graze my forehead as he speaks.

I tilt my face upwards to find his honey eyes firmly locked on me. They smoulder like embers, burning with desire. It's enough to make my cheeks, my ear tips blush. My perilous level of curiosity has always been my downfall, but for once I embrace it.

If this is to be my last night before my world comes crumbling down, then I wish to spend it with him. I long to know what it is like to be wanted for *who* I am, not just *what* I am.

With his binding words broken, I do not *need* him anymore. I do not need anyone. Yet I cannot deny I *want* him. And maybe it's okay to want something that isn't good for you. He wants his wars and rum, and I, I want him.

"I meant it before, but not anymore. Something's changed," I admit quietly.

The same look of passion he has for conquering islands is now staring me down. And much like the way he jumped off the cliff, he does not hesitate for even the briefest of seconds. I'm beginning to think he doesn't know how to.

He strikes like lightning, pressing his opened mouth against mine. Hot and crackling with electricity.

A yelp of surprise escapes my lips before he occupies them completely. His hands are calloused from wielding swords and hauling boat ropes, but his lips are velvety soft. Dangerously inviting.

Much like lightning, there is a pause after the glorious entrance. I break for air and he pauses, scanning my face to ensure nothing is wrong. And for the first time in forever, there isn't anything wrong.

This is the moment of silence where the thunder decides its fate. How close to the lightning do I follow?

I stretch onto my tiptoes and dive right after him, planting a hasty, inexperienced kiss on his waiting lips. I worry about my technique, but I feel his grin.

Together we may be a thunderstorm, but Zeus doesn't seem to mind the competition.

He lifts me in a smooth motion and perches me on the windowsill. His body pushes against mine. My knees fall apart. My heart paces.

Wrapping my thighs around his waist, I pull him in closer. With trembling hands, I remove his knife from his waistband. He freezes for a second until I toss it aside, grabbing fistfuls of his shirt instead. I untuck it his slacks and tug it over his head in a single movement.

A thin golden chain hangs around his neck, housing one of his mother's broaches. It lays nestled on his toned, bare chest.

With his torso and window holding me in place, his hands are free to roam. His hot palms inch their way along the insides of my thighs. A soft moan escapes my mouth.

The glass pane behind me trembles, followed by a crack sound.

He breaks away from my lips, chuckling softly, "Wow, a few kisses and you're almost shattering windows. I can only imagine the destruction you'd cause if we-"

"Shh," I chastise, and lightly slap his torso.

Scooting off the ledge, I twist around to examine a three-inch crack in the corner pane. Beyond the crack, through the window and across the bay I see something far more damaging.

The calm seas of moments ago have been replaced with choppy, dark tides slamming against each other without pattern or natural flow.

I place an open palm against the cold glass. I feel it first as vibrations immediately meet my touch, but then I hear it. A high-pitch scream begins to register in my ears.

"Is something wrong?" Kellan asks.

The cry grows louder in volume, higher in pitch. Almost as if it's bubbling up from underwater, screaming its way to the surface.

"Can't you hear that?"

He shakes his head and scans my face with wide eyes. Gods above, it's like the hippocampi all over again. He cannot hear the magic screams that I can, but I somehow doubt his harpooning arm can save me this time.

Another crack springs in the top hand corner of the window, shattering the entire square pane. The sea's shriek comes flooding in along with winter wind. Just when I thought it couldn't get any bloody louder.

A spiderweb of fractures races along the glass.

Shit.

"Get down!" Kellan roars, as he slams me onto the cobbled floor beneath us. In an instant, he towers his body over mine as the window explodes. Glass shards rain from above. The sudden gust quenches all the candles, plummeting the room into darkness.

"Are you okay?" I yell over the piercing note.

He says something, but I cannot hear him. I hear nothing but the monstrous din. I roll out from the cage of his body, shake off the debris and stumble my way to my feet.

Kellan's back is in tatters.

Countless slits score every inch of his pale skin. Mauve droplets race down his spine as he stands upright. He winces and shakes shards free from the poultice on his forearm.

With my fleeting moment of happiness over, the guilt returns.

He keeps getting injured and it's all my fault. Even a son of Ares isn't robust enough for the chaos of my life.

I planned to confront the sea in the morning, but like most of my plans it didn't work out my way.

The sea has come for me. *She* has come for me.

I don't waste a second longer trying to decode what Kellan is saying. Nothing he could say could stop me now. I turn on my heel and sprint out of the cottage.

TWENTY

Sprinting down the stone steps, I barrel my way towards the bay. The howling gale whisking through the streets has extinguished the once glowing lanterns of the party, plunging the town into an eerie shade.

The gold and bronze bunting has been ripped free from its tether and now flails wildly through the air. The hum of laughter and chatter I wished to crack my door open to hear is now gone. It has been replaced with the hushed worried tones of islanders wondering if they should catch a glimpse of the commotion or hide under their beds.

The moment my feet land on the dock, the shrieking stops. Instead, a frantic disturbance begins. A wide whirl starts in the centre of the bay, and as I get closer, I realise what I'm approaching. My mouth falls wide open. My knees lock, freezing me to the spot.

It's Charybdis.

The seas most infamous monstrous messenger. It seems my mother had upped her tactics since the hippocampi messengers.

It unhinges its circular jaw. With its immense mouth gaped open, the icy waters flood inward. Swirling its numerous black tongues in the water, the beast causes a vortex. Through the heart of the whirlpool the beast bursts upright. It rises, higher and higher until its infinite rows of teeth nor its dozens of beady eyes are visible anymore. All I see is the impenetrable, ebony scales laying flush against the creature's lengthy body. The equivalent of armour in the sea.

The people who opted to creep closer and catch a glimpse are now screaming. Bloodcurdling, terrifying screams I know will be heard on the neighbouring isles across the cove.

Although I understand their sheer terror, I try not to feel it myself. The beast in the bay is completely petrifying I agree, but it is a creature of Poseidon just like me. Theoretically, it should do me no harm, but I've much closer relatives who want to destroy me, so I best not test the theory right now.

Having reached its zenith, the Charybdis begins the delivery. The sea spews forth from its gaping mouth, pouring out every side like a living fountain. Water cascades down its slinky sides, allowing pools of saliva and seafoam to merge into the bay.

With one almighty heave, the creature belches out a huge tidal wave. The real reason the monster came is now hurtling towards me on its wave which snaps the masts of nearby ships as if they were toothpicks.

An oyster shell so large it could have birthed Aphrodite mounts the pier with the wave. It slides down each wooden slat, scarring it along the way until it grinds to a wobbly halt at my bare feet.

"Wren," Kellan bellows from somewhere behind me, "Get back from there."

He shouts in a voice dripping with authority, that is hard to refuse. But thankfully I have weeks of practice annoying him, and years of practice ignoring royalty. I don't turn around to see his sullen face when I move forward, but I feel it.

I run my palms along the shell's bumpy strata until my fingers locate the hinge. Ignoring his protests, I lever my fingertips between the two halves. Sharp shale nicks the skin between my fingers instantly.

I brace myself with a shaky deep breath and prise the weighted shell open.

There's a moment of silence.

Then the chaos begins.

An unholy banshee scream erupts from the cockle of the shell. Except this is no banshee. The cries are far too familiar. The voice echoing all around is Dove's. Her ethereal, delicate tone bellows an ungodly roar; one I know she could not produce without great pain.

A level of pain I know she could not survive, because no one could, not even her with all her strength and selflessness.

The bloodcurdling scream suddenly cuts. The shell snaps shut, and the reptilian giant slinks back into the deep, knowing its duty is done.

The splash from the descending beast sends a last wave towards the deck. It makes its impact at the same time as my collapsing knees.

She killed Dove.

My one and only friend; gone. I had always wished Dove could take my place and carry out the Luring Ritual first, but I never in an immortal lifetime thought she would ever take the brunt of my mothers' wrath. I never thought the Queen would murder one of her own subjects just to hurt me.

I'm sobbing hot tears when a cold hand grips my shoulder.

"Only the Queen of the Water World, and Seven Spikes can control Charybdis," Kellan says flatly.

Digging his fingers around my collarbone, he hauls me upright from the sodden planks. His glaring eyes demanding a hundred answers without posing a single question. He forces me to look at the anger I've ignited in him, the fury I've sparked in yet another person.

"For someone who cannot lie you certainly know how to withhold the truth, don't you?" he snaps, clenching and unclenching his free fist, "When you said you were afraid of your mother...."

I cannot answer.

I cannot open my mouth. I just stare at the shell, the screams it let escape still repeating in my head.

Kellan shakes me roughly, "Answer me. Is your mother the Queen?"

I nod my head, which sends tears flying.

As Callum and Fletcher come running onto the dock, Kellan drops his hold of me and paces away.

"What in Hel is that?" Callum exclaims, placing a protective arm on Fletcher to stop him inching forward.

"It resembles a messenger shell from Charybdis, but that beast solely serves the..."

Fletcher's voice trails off as his sight locks onto me. A long, calculating silence endures. He turns his attention to his King who is frantically pacing the dock and refusing to look at me.

Fletcher is a smart man, too smart at times. He could be Master of the Tomes if he preferred.

Callum whips his head frantically between his husband and I, "Can someone explain what's going on?"

Kellan ceases his pacing. He stands before me with his chest rising rapidly as he draws short, furious breaths.

"Wren is the fucking Princess of the Water World and the Seven Spikes," Kellan shouts, "And her Queenly mother is ripping up half the sea looking for her, threatening to drown my bloody archipelago."

Callum turns to stand shoulder to shoulder with his brother, his face looking equally as livid, "Was this your plan? To have you infiltrate from the land and her from the sea?"

"*Infiltrate?* I was taken from the sea to save you," I exclaim, throwing my arms into the air, "And I have zero interest in your bloody islands. I tried to leave here. *Twice.* But he won't let me!"

I point my finger like a sword towards Kellan, but he does not respond nor flinch. He simply stares at me whilst grinding his jaw back and forth.

"Well he isn't stopping you now, so leave." Callum turns and throws a wide, open arm to the sea, "Maybe if you go home, she won't attack us."

Go home.

Something catches in my throat. I was just beginning to feel like here could be my home instead.

"What is it your mother wants?" Fletcher asks once he's finally shaken off his stunned expression.

"She wants me to rule beside her and remain within the Seven Spikes Queendom...forever. She demands I embrace my immortal syren life. It's almost time for my Luring Lullaby ceremony. She sees it as a sign of loyalty to the Queendom, and a promise of what is to come, but I do not want to partake. I cannot. I do not want to kill innocent men."

I do not want to kill Kellan, I add mentally.

"You had no problem slaughtering the Soleil Island men," Callum says flatly.

"Enough," Kellan snaps, and throws a look at his brother, "You would not be here without her. None of us would be if she had not defeated the Soleil men. Their deaths are on my hands, not hers. But *you*..."

He steps closer to me, shaking his head, "You should have told me who you are."

I untuck my hair to cover my face, and with as much bitterness as I can muster ask, "Why, would you have flung me back to the sea and caught yourself a different syren?"

He wraps a tense arm around my waist, pulls me forward and releases a long and staggered sigh, "No, never. I was fated to find you, even if you are a pain in the ass."

"I did not take you as a man to believe in fate."

He places his heavy head atop my crown and sighs, "I'm usually not, but when I dreamt of you every night after Alistair took my siblings, I took it as a sign. Although you were less sassy and had wings in my dreams."

"You dreamt of me?"

A nodding Fletcher catches my eye, "He wouldn't shut up about it. I tried to explain syrens hadn't possessed feathers in decades, but he paid no heed to me, as usual."

Kellan mutters a curse into my hair before explaining, "I would not shut up about it because it was like no dream I had ever had. It was a message from the gods, I am sure of it."

"Like an omen?" I ask.

"Why do you ask?" he pressed, knowing there was more to be said. He was getting far too good at knowing when I left things unsaid and I was growing tired of half-truths.

"I had an omen dream about you the time I broke the table leg in the cottage. You were the man I had to perform my ritual on."

A sly grin slowly cracks across his serious face, and he winks at me as if we're the only two people in the world,

"Is the thought of lying with me upon your coral bed that nightmare-inducing?"

I smack his chest, knowing my cheeks are burning lilac under the gaping stares of Fletcher and Callum, "It never got that far. My song failed to work on you, and when I couldn't bear it anymore, the Queen punctured your heart with the Trident."

He sobers and his cocky grin fades.

Callum clears his throat. He has been unusually quiet for a few moments, just staring at the sliver of space between his brother and me. With a high arching eyebrow, similar to that when he saw me stumbling out of Kellan's bed, his face asks a thousand questions his sealed mouth does not. It was one of the few differences between the brothers.

"Well what does it mean? He dreams of you saving our family, yet you dream of your family destroying us. What is going to happen?"

The emphasis he places on *destroying us* causes me to flinch. I swallow hard and glance at the waiting face of each man surrounding me. I cannot ask them to partake in a fight the gods themselves have planned. It's unfair to pit this fragile family that has already been through so much into yet another battle, one they know nothing about.

"Wren?" Kellan presses me for an answer.

"Just *shh* for a moment, I'm thinking," I mutter, although realistically I know I'm stalling to buy more time. Because I have to tell them what I'm up against, who I'm up against, and more importantly, who I am.

I close my eyes, unable to watch the fury I'm about to ignite in yet another soul.

"...And I was meant to go to the Eastern Acropolis to pray to the gods and find out how to defeat my mother, but when I resurfaced, I was bound to Kellan by the bloody binding oath. See time passes differently in the Water World, and I thought I'd have more time but my mother must have figured out Dove's ruse immediately, and well now's she's coming here and I still have no idea what Poseidon expects me to do!"

I finish my rambling and brace for the onslaught on shouts, but I hear none.

Peering one eye open, I glance down to find Kellan on bended knee. Fletcher kneels beside him, and Callum stares at me with wide eyes before Fletcher grabs a fistful of fabric from his slacks and tugs him downward into a kneeling stance too.

"You once asked me if Kellan was a demi-god," Fletcher says, although I wish he hadn't, Kellan will *never* let that go, "I didn't think to pose the question to you, Goddess."

"Oh, for the love of the gods, I'm still me!" I sigh, grappling at Fletcher's arms to haul him up, "Still the stubborn syren you strapped a bridle onto to shut up."

Fletcher visibly pales, unsure whether he should start grovelling or running for any past actions. Callum flops out of his kneel and sits on the ground instead, looking physically and figuratively, floored. And Kellan remains on one knee, staring up at me with raw admiration and reverence. It takes all my might to not point and laugh.

My momentary smirk is wiped away with the sheets of rain begin to fall from the Heavens. A heavy metallic scent starts to waft through all the bay. Brewing a storm was just the start of my mother's display.

Catching Kellan by the scruff, I pull him up but of course he's too muscular for me to budge him an inch. Thankfully, he raises himself, standing toe-to-toe with me.

"This isn't a coin toss you'll win," I explain.

He opens to mouth to challenge me but shut it again and pauses, "Well, if it's my Fate to lose than I'll be defeated in battle. I'd rather perish with honour than a clean knife."

I shake my head, "But I don't-"

"Together, or not all at still stands, Wren," he interrupts with a cutting tone.

A single raindrop dripping from his nose is the only movement on his stern, hardened face, "I won't tether you to a mainmast, or confine you to a cabin, I know this is your fight, your destiny. But it is mine too. I won't hold you back this time, instead I'll have your back. Whatever you need."

"Me too," Fletcher adds softly. Callum remains cross-armed but stiffly nods.

Tears that I've barely regained control of manage to escape. I pray the downfall is masks them as I'd hate to shatter the Goddess illusion so quickly by my blubbering like a scared infant.

"How long until she arrives?" Fletcher asks, ever practical.

I crane my neck to examine the skies above. Dark, stormy clouds are rolling in, blowing seagulls off-course.

"Half an hour?" I offer, but it's drowned out by the crack of lightning striking the bay.

Shit.

"Probably less," I gulp.

TWENTY-ONE

A plan of action is quickly drawn up. Kellan fetches his bell from the privy council meeting and finds Ludwig.

"You're the fastest sprinter I know. I need you to run across the bridges to Meteorite Spit and Star Spike and tell everyone to come to the town square."

"What if they don't listen to me?"

"Tell them you're the new Herald of the King, then they will listen. Now go!"

Ludwig bows before sprinting off towards the neighbouring isles. The bell ringing in his hand as he flees.

"What is the plan for when we've gathered the people?" Fletcher asks.

We're jogging side by side to keep up with the brothers as they barrel their way through the docks.

Kellan looks at me over his shoulder and shrugs, "Ask her, she's the expert. Wren, how does one defend themselves against a syren attack?"

I fall silent which causes everyone to abruptly stop walking. Their anticipating faces growing more uneasy by the passing wordless seconds.

Think, Wren, think.

"What lies beyond the cottage? At the very top of those bastard steps?" I ask.

"The Virginal Temple of Athena?" Callum asks with a raised brow.

A Temple? *Perfect!*

"Usher everyone up there. It's hopefully high enough on the hill it won't be drowned, and with any luck, it could block out most of the sound," I explain, "Order every harpist and lyre player you can to perform as loud as they can. They are to keep playing until they're told otherwise. They do not stop. I do not care if their fingers are worn down to the bone, it's the only hope we have of keeping your citizens sane. Is there stained glass in this Temple?"

Fletcher nods enthusiastically, "Oh yes, tons of it! It's beautiful, a true work of art-

"It's all going to shatter," Kellan interrupts Fletcher's awe, vaulting himself into the docked boat before us, "Tell Shelli to bring as many reams of her fabric as she has. Hammer them into the window frames and sills to stop shards exploding into the Temple."

I wince, knowing his advice is from personal and very recent experience. The way he subtly rolls his shoulders tells me he's thinking of it too. I didn't get a decent look at the cuts on his back, but I knew they would need to be tended to soon, along with whatever other injuries lie before us.

"And tie the doors shut to stop citizens being lured to the bay," Kellan adds, pulling ropes loose on the boat and dumping them in a pile on the deck.

"The last thing we need is the entire town chasing Wren or her mummy dearest," Callum mutters, before turning his attention to the sailors who have gathered on the pier.

The men are quickly sent to work, gathering harpoons, bows and arrows, and anything else that could be fashioned into a weapon from the other boats. I do not have it in me to tell them it's a futile task, so I let them feel as if they are being productive. I figure it's best to stay busy when certain doom is impending.

I step into the boat with Kellan and start winding the piles of ropes into neat reams, "Someone with ichor in their veins should stay with the people to watch over them."

"Callum," Kellan hollers without even pausing for a beat, "You're staying in the Temple with our people. Aveen has to be guarded."

Callum's intense stare burns into Kellan's back who is too busy collecting harpoons to notice nor care. So, he moves his gaze to me, "If anything happens to my brother, I will kill you."

He may not be a syren, but I trust Callum spits the truth at me. He storms off towards the mass of people ascending the hill towards the Temple, leaving Kellan and me alone on the rocky boat.

Gulping, I turn my attention to him, "I think you should follow him-

"No," he cuts me off, "I meant what I said, together or not at all. Although the "not at all" option has been denied. If she wishes to rise against me let her try. We will trounce her. Together."

The half an hour I anticipated we would have to prepare, turned out to be far too generous. My mother always hated tardiness.

Not long after the Temple doors are shut, I sense her surfacing. The sea itself vibrates as a band of about thirty sirens break through the waves. They form a wall along the curvature of the bay, linking their arms and splaying out their tailfins in a defence display.

Although they remain silent as their gills retract, the bay is filled with an eerie melody. The rumble of thunder is starkly contrasted by the upbeat folk melodies carried downward from the Temple upon the winter wind.

In the centre of the cove where the Charybdis slinked back into the sea, now comes an equally terrifying sight. In a commotion of ripples and bubbles, a hippocampus canters through the waves, carrying the Queen atop its rump.

Seeing her without the ridiculously long tail skirt makes her look marginally less imposing. But of course, there's a reason for her change of wardrobe. She's unwilling to be vulnerable in the time it would take to shed the skirt, so instead, she came prepared. No tail, no gills.

Rather than beach herself, she sacrifices the hippocampus. With a whip woven from stiff seagrass, she drives the beast relentlessly forward until it reaches the shoreline.

Once its scaly hooves clop on the sand, she continues kicking its sides with her shark tooth spurs, forcing the creature to haul its hefty, muscular rear-end across the sodden sand. It manages a dozen painful-looking strides before its front legs buckle under the pressure and it lands in a heap.

Never in my wildest nightmares did I think the bellowing cry of a hippocampus would ever elicit sympathy within me, but as my mother steps off the beast and gives it a solid kick to the jaw before walking away, I find myself flinching.

With her shoulders arched back and head held high, one could almost overlook the wobbly in her unsteady legs as they reacquaint themselves with gravity and soil for the first time in decades. With each step she takes, I am more and more convinced my insides have been replaced with a labyrinth of serpents.

Kellan selects up a longbow from the pile and bounces its weight in his hold.

The Queen stalls in her approach but offers a raised eyebrow, "Typical Descendant of Ares attitude to reach for a weapon before offering a greeting."

"Greetings are offered to those who are welcome," Kellan retorts simply, but I hear his breath catch in his throat slightly.

This is his first time seeing her, and I'm sure our striking similarity is catching him off guard. I'm used to us looking so alike, but the sight of her takes me back too. For the first time in my life, I look older than her. And since that pinnacle apex in our ageing has been passed, it can never be reverted. I have officially outgrown her.

"I'm sure you can gather I'm here to commandeer these isles," she offers, throwing a light hand to her creatures waiting to pounce in the bay, "A man with your lineage ought to know how this process works. Your father took stole these isles, and you stole Soleil so I'm sure the concept is familiar to you."

"Alistair stole from me first," Kellan argues, sounding far too like his sister. I hoped he would know better than to try to win an argument with someone like her.

I want to say something, anything to her, but it's as if I've forgotten how to speak.

"Ah," the Queen offers with a wide smile, "Well if that is the criteria you deem necessary for an island seizure, I do believe *you* stole *my* daughter first."

"I'm not yours anymore," I finally spit out once I've remembered how to form words.

"Why because you found yourself a new master?" She spits the remark at Kellan but keeps her constant and disgusted stare on me.

"Wren belongs to no-one," he snaps.

"We'll see about that."

The faintest flick of her wrist is all it takes for the Queen begins to orchestrate the symphony of syrens.

The alto syrens begin humming their deep note to produce the thunder of the sea. Lightning cracks overhead, and I doubt it's a coincidence.

The soprano singers join in once, and the chanting begins; *Ela se emás, éla se emás, Ola mazí, ola mazí.*

Come to us, come to us, all at once, all at once.

As they begin to harmonise, the music begins to swell, vibrating the already electric air all around us. I expect them to project their voices across the bay as we're taught to, but instead, their tune is directed towards the waves themselves. The only face I see is Rhea's. She mouths the word, *Sorry*, before continuing her chant.

There's a gigantic disturbance in the water halting most of the singing syrens. Waves smack against nearby rocks as water is displaced by something deep down below. A grin unfolded across my mother's face, as a plump, slithering body breaches the water.

Ugh, I pray to the gods she has not brought a plague of eels with her.

A flash of lightning splits the sky, as the beast splits the water. As it unfolds itself from beneath the waves, water rushes off its endless blank scales.

Through the darkness and sheets of rain I cannot make out its form, but due its limbs and size, it's *definitely not* an eel.

Another flash of lightning illuminates the beast.

"Is that..." Kellan's roar trails off as we are cast into shadow from the monster.

"Hydra." I gulp.

With its distinctive multiple heads and stench of death, suddenly a plague of eels seemed like a blessing. Unlike Charybdis, Hydra is no creature of Poseidon. It has no loyalty to me or syrens in general. I shiver to think of the compromise my mother came to with Echidna to borrow her most prized and beastly creation.

"What did you sacrifice to the gods this time?" I roar across the bay, the wind carrying my voice towards the syrens, "You already gave up our wings! Would you risk us losing our voices too? Would you rather we be mute like you?"

The syren symphony of moments ago is now an outcry of shock and horror. Their song turns into shouts of anger as they feel the truth in my words. But it's too late, the Queen has already used their powers for what she needed.

As Hydra heaves its sodden body and multiple heads from the bay, the water level lowers rapidly. Boats sink into the sodden sand beneath them, anchors now fully visible. Coy fish who cannot react quick enough are left flopping for their lives on the freshly exposed silt.

Kellan knocks an arrow and takes aim for the beast which stands obediently behind my mother. The arrow soars through the frigid air before bouncing off the creature's rump and landing at the Queens's feet instead.

Loud, gargling laughter which sounds worse than the scream of a hippocampus erupts from her thin lips.

"Your self-belief would almost be amusing if it were not so misplaced," she guffaws.

Whoosh.

An arrow I didn't even see him draw, whips past my ear and lands *splat* in the shoulder of the Queen. She manages to stay upright, but it wipes the smirk clean off her face.

Knowing the accuracy he showed harpooning the hippocampi on a moving boat, there was no way he missed his target whilst on steady ground standing this close. I've no doubt his warning shot was fired out of respect for her being related to me, but one we all could assume his next arrow would land slightly higher, and two inches to the left, directly in the centre of her gullet.

Wrapping her long, slender fingers around the feathered base of the arrow, she yanks it free from her skin in a single motion. Blood runs freely from the wound, and its colour stuns me still. Her blood was not rich with ichor like mine. If anything, it resembles that of a Descendant. It holds far more mortal crimson than I ever suspected, but how was I to know?

The Queen never bled.

It was a sign of weakness, and no one ever got close enough to hurt her. Until now.

"Dove was right," I stutter, "About everything. The gods gave me more ichor than you. I'm more powerful."

Her jaw tightens as she grinds her teeth, "I begged the gods for a blessing, yet all I got was a curse. I may have received you from Poseidon himself, but I won't hesitate to fling you to Hades."

As Kellan knocks another arrow, a dark shadow falls on us as the Hydra looms above, eager for the hunt.

"*Tóra!*" she shouts, releasing the beast upon us.

Hydra swings its neck like a mace flail, whipping one of its heads towards us. Its unhinged jaw drags along the wooden slats as it barrels its bared teeth in our direction.

Kellan drops his bow and grabs my wrist instead, dragging me along as he bolts.

He leaps off the pier, landing hard in the sand and pulling me along with him. We sprint, kicking up a mound of sodden sand. I run harder, and kick up more grit, hoping some of it will land in its eye. I hunch up my shoulders as the breath of the beast lands on my neck and sends shivers down my spine. I keep my legs moving but I close my eyes, bracing to feel its teeth chomp me in half.

An ungodly wail rips through the bay. The head chasing us, suddenly rolls in front of our path, forcing us to skid to a halt.

The gigantic head wobbles on the spot like one of Kellan's spinning coins before it lands to one side. Its spindly neck trails onto the sand beside it, flopping as its nerve ending come to terms with being severed. A puddle of black ichor oozes in its wake.

"No!" My mother roars, "You stupid mortal!"

I twist to find Callum panting hard where we just stood on the pier. Wielding a long silver sword, he cranes his neck to look at neck he just severed. Above him, the exposed arteries he slit, rain black ichor. He stands firmly in its shower, seeming unphased and already beginning to hack his weapon at the next head.

My mother, Kellan and I all bolt towards him in unison.

"Stop it, Callum!" I bellow.

My mother might be nearer to him, but the weight of gravity has made her sluggish, and her legs are weakened from years of minimal use. That, and I'm pretty sure Kellan is the fastest man in all the realms.

He ducks under the flailing head, slides between Hydra's legs. Barely missing the clamouring feet, he burst out by the rear of the creature, leap over its tail and slams into his brother. They crash into the ground, and roll twice, knocking Callum's sword out of reach.

It happened so fast, but it's still too late.

The Hydra's neck throbs a few times before the gaping flesh begins to knit back together. But the healing doesn't stop there. Its skin and scales continue to grow, buckling and contorting to form two bumps.

As Hydra draws in an unending, furious breath, the lumps inflate like sails catching the wind. Before I have time to catch my breath, the beast has donned two more heads.

All its onyx eyes lock onto the brothers sprawled out on the ground, just beneath its panting chest.

"*Tóra, Hydra, tóra!*" My mother shouts at the beast, commanding it to attack once again. She may not have a singing voice, but she can certainly bellow orders.

The Hydra flings open all seven jaws and takes aim for the brothers. Kellan grabs Callum by the collar, hauling him along as they struggle to find their feet.

"Where's Aveen?" Kellan roars. His tight grip around Callum's neck now seeming more threatening than supportive.

"She's at the Temple. I gave her a sword, she'll be fine!" Callum retorts, as they continue their race towards me. Hydra snapping its endless jaws at their ankles.

Kellan tries to snag a hold of me as he blasts past, but I yank my arm away.

"I have an idea!" I bellow as I begin to run in the direction nobody is expecting.

Weaving under the heads of the beast, I sprint towards the water's edge which now lies a hundred feet further away than before.

Thankfully, the steep steps of these isles have finally proved good for something as my legs are better equipped to handle the immense pressure.

With each pounding step, I stamp down my rising sense of doubt. As the lapping waves slap against my ankles, I turn to face Hydra.

The beast is halfway between Kellan and me, which is entirely the wrong place for any enemy to be.

Banishing any uncertainty from my core, I muster every drop of courage I have in my fellow syrens, but also myself.

"Help me, *adelfés!*" I cry, "Lure it back!"

Hydra falters for a moment. Unsure which opponent is more urgent to attack, half its heads stare in my direction, the rest face the brothers who are collecting weapons from the pile the sailors made.

"*Ela se emás, éla se emás!*" I roar towards Hydra, snapping all seven heads to focus on me. It no longer falters. It charges towards me.

Its glossy eyes are glaring and fully focused. This monster isn't being lured to me; it's just planning to kill me of its own accord. I continue to shriek my chant, faster and louder than before but "*Ela se emás*" is a choir chorus. Screaming "come to *us*", won't work if I'm the only fool singing it.

With its gigantic weight vibrating the ground as it nears, my knees being to shake, and I threaten to fall at its mercy. Perhaps fear is making me hallucinate, but I swear I hear a seraph's angelic voice break through the thunder. It bounces off the waves and rocks, ringing in my ears. This sickeningly sweet song will be the last I hear in this realm. I expect to hear the heralds trumpets of death any second.

To the left of the cove, Callum and Kellan fight back to back with the harpies diving from overhead. To the right, stands my mother, with a repugnant grin visible from here. She's all too delighted to see me fail, to see me die.

"Do as our Queen asks!" The angel voice demands.

I turn to find Rhea, orchestrating her fellow syrens into groups. Within seconds my chant is being reciprocated.

The mantra quickens. The harmonies swell.

Hydra shakes all its heads furiously as if to rid its mind of the din, but its eyes gradually glaze over as the luring takes hold. The same soulless fogged stare I observed in the Soleil men now washed over the beast.

I continue to shout the words, although optimism has heightened my pitch. The words run frantically from my lips until I cannot hear individual syllables anymore. Hydra looms closer until I stand between its front legs, shaking but still shouting. Its heads droop towards me, although in a sleepy manner this time instead of hunger.

As Hydra sinks its front feet into the water, the chant hits its crescendo. It's the loudest chorus I've ever heard. Windows and glass from every corner the isles, shatter in unison.

"Continue, but ease *adelfés,*" I instruct, knowing the Temple would be windowless and more vulnerable now. Distance, merry folk music continues to drift towards us on the winter breeze. I know if I can hear them, they can probably hear us.

Obediently, the syrens lower the heads and their tone. With a seductive and irresistible whisper, they call forth the beast, who's now up to its belly in waves.

As the tip of the beast's tail slinks into the water, I return my attention to my mother.

She's panting hard, lips pursed with pure hatred. Losing Hydra will earn her a place in Echidna's bad books, the result of which would be eternal servitude, but she also just lost something much more personal.

Rhea calling me her Queen shows an irrevocable change causing my mother to lose her people, her title and her Queendom. I want to tell her she should not fear

the wrath of Echidna as she won't live to see the dawn,
but she's already barrelling towards the brothers.

TWENTY-TWO

Unlike my fellow syrens, harpies remain loyal to the owner of the crown until the point of death. My mother might not be able to sing, and harpies might be resistant to luring, but she has enough magic mind-control and allegiance to use them as her last weapon.

Keeping a safe distance, my mother flails her arms wildly as she acts like a puppet-master, ordering harpies to dive and rise at her command. She locks her eyes onto Kellan's bandaged arm and sees a golden opportunity.

I'm almost halfway to the brothers when my mother orders another harpy to dive. The bird-bodied minion burrows her sharp talons straight into the raw flesh on Kellan's forearm. He crumples to the ground in a ball, tucking his arm under him as he roars.

His wail of pain sparks action from Callum instantly. He snags the left-wing of the creature and hauls her to the ground with relative ease given its smaller stature. She flaps her wings wildly once she hits the silt, twisting and contorting in every direction.

The harpies nestmate seizes Callum's jacket by the scruff and starts dragging him away. He is too heavy for her to take flight with, but she manages to drag him, kicking and roaring down most of the pier.

"No, leave him be!" I cry, seeing my mother raise her hand to summon another harpy.

Kellan rolls onto side and somehow stumbles to his feet. His forearm wound has reopened and is even deeper than before. Even on this cold, winter night, sweat beads his paling forehead. He retrieves his knife from his waistband, but with his deteriorating arm lying limp by his side, he's forced to wield it using his non-dominate hand.

He spits out a mouthful of sand, draws a staggering pant, and roars, "Well, come on then. Give it your bloody best!"

My mother keeps her left hand held high as if it were tethered to the harpies hovering overhead. In her right hand firmly gripped around the Trident, and on her face, a toothsome grin as she enjoys every second of the tension.

It makes me want to vomit, but I continue running, and she allows me this false hope. She lets me believe I'll get there in time, that I'll be able to save him.

"Kestrel, no!" I say, "It's me you want, not him."

She turns eerily smoothly, as if underwater, and stares me down.

It seems speaking her name aloud for the first time in my life caught her attention. It shocks me too. I can scarcely believe I even remembered it, but then again being named after a non-singing, bird of prey known for stealing the homes of others is a great memory jogger.

Her grin falters for a moment before she raises a sarcastic eyebrow, "You don't *honestly* want me to release the harpies on you instead of him, now do you? You're normally more selfish than that."

She has a point, and that's why her taunt stings so damn much.

"Please," I beg, "He can't get hurt because of me anymore."

She shrugs once before silently dropping her arm. The harpies descend in a swarm of chaos and feathers straight in my direction.

Talons wrap around my calf, immediately hauling me back across the bay. Silt, sand, and saltwater chafe at my exposed skin. The stinging sensation is so intense when another harpy seizes my arms to soar me into the air, I feel relieved.

My fleeting reprieve is dashed away, as the winged creatures continue to ascend. Higher and higher, with no obvious direction except upwards.

Everything seems slower from up here, but the rate in which my mother runs Trident-first towards the Kellan is still too fast. Through the sheets of rain and my sodden hair clinging to my face, I catch a glimpse of a shiny metal object cascading through the air. But I cannot make out of it's the Trident or Kellan's knife.

The harpies don't slow once they reach the thick rainclouds suffocating the sky, instead, they beat their wings harder and blast straight through.

Suddenly I can't breathe. Maybe it's the dense humidity of the air or the thinness of the altitude, but realistically it's the fact I now have a clear view of where the harpies are lugging me towards.

The protruding juts of rock that cause Fletcher and Kellan to hold their breaths, now wait for me a hundred feet below my dangling frame.

The same sharp shale that split my arm and almost killed me days ago was finally going to finish the job.

Great.

The howling gale is too great for me to turn my neck any other way. The cruel wind burns my eyes, forcing me to stare upon my doomed fate. I'm about to curse Zephyrus and his blasted gusts, when it offers me the smallest salvation.

"Ares!" Kellan's roar to his god carries upwards towards me and the skies, "You save her, hear me? Gods damnit, save her!"

His cry sounds less like a prayer, and more a demand, but perhaps the gods will find amusement in his tone. At least I know he's alive, furious as usual, but alive.

Without notice, the harpies release me.

There is no beginning. I'm already hurtling downwards before I think. My clothes flap wildly against my thrashing limbs. The sky swallows me whole, somehow smothering me and rejecting me at the same time as it offers me up to the rocks below.

Wincing, I brace for the inevitable. Any second now, my frame will smash into oblivion. I will be no more.

I impact against nothing, yet a burning rip tears across my back. My shoulder blades buckle as if they're being pulled through my skin.

The raw scream to Poseidon I release is so unending it causes my gills to rupture open. My body's instinctual act of self-preservation seems futile; I'm pretty sure my lungs have fallen out my back. There is nothing left inside except this pain.

I never made it to the Eastern Acropolis, but perhaps I could make them come to me. I think they owe it to me after bestowing me such an arduous life.

Lightning splits the skies. Bright, pure light saturates even my closed lids as if it were welcoming me to the spirit realm.

Gods above how haven't I hit the damn spikes yet?

Forcing my eyes open, I see the rocks do not loom closer anymore. Instead, I'm suspended mid-air.

I gulp and twist to see if the harpies have caught me. Perhaps this is a game of torment they're playing, the way orca's toy with their prey.

Glancing over my shoulder, I find something far more terrifying. The scene makes me cry out to Poseidon once more.

Two long, lustrous wings protrude from my shoulder blades and beat slow, steadying flaps to keep me hovering.

"What the Hel!" I cry, twisting and turning as I attempt to shake them off. They do not budge. They remain steadfast.

With a banshee squawk, the harpies bow their heads to me before taking off for the horizon.

My legs kick frantically as I dangle mid-air.

From this height, the destruction is clearly visible. Callum lays slumped across a wooden support beam for the pier. He is either dead or unconscious. I pray it's the latter.

Kellan is struggling to lift something from the ground. It's hefty and...steaming?

My mother squirms away from him like a damn coral snake. She inches her way towards the shoreline. Shame for her she'll never reach it.

I should have no idea how to utilise my wings, yet I do. My song, my gills and now my feathers are all gifts from Poseidon.

I was born, no, *crafted*, for this.

TWENTY-THREE

Rolling my stiff shoulders, I stretch out my arms wide, allowing wind to unfurl my wings to the furthest degree. I take a final breath, then dive towards them.

Like the stars above I spent so much of my life gazing at, I blaze across the sky like a meteorite.

As I near Kellan, it becomes obvious what it's straining to hoist onto this ravaged arm. It's a sturdy shield. Not just any shield, but the Armour of Ares.

It must have come down with the lightning bolt I saw! Steaming, and still glowing hot in places he straps the metal plate onto his arm and holds it in front of his chest.

I spot the Trident discarded on the ground, and suddenly an idea comes to mind.

A tuning fork!

Swooping low to the ground, I snatch the iron handle as I soar past.

"Kellan!" I cry, my cheeks wobbling with the sheer force of flight. I come in fast towards him, so fast I don't think I'll ever stop.

Most people, mortal or magic, would quake at the sight of an open gilled, screaming syren, flying straight for them whilst wielding a weapon of the gods, but thankfully Kellan isn't most people.

His eyes grow wide, but he stands his ground. He bends his knees, bracing for the blow and tucks his face behind the armour.

With as much force as I can, I smack the Trident into the centre of the Shield.

The impact blows us both backwards in a flash of blinding light.

The purest resonance I've ever heard escalates in pitch until it's so high I hear nothing at all. From the vibration rattling the bones inside my palms, I know the Trident is still reverberating its tune, yet silence bellows across the bay.

There is only one clear noise interrupting the peace, and that's Kestrel. Squealing and squirming on the sand as she tries to defend herself from the sound.

I haul myself upright, using the pole of the Trident to steady my steps as my heavy wings threaten to tip me off balance.

Just like when she sent the hippocampi to torment me, this is a song only she can hear. Except this symphony comes straight from the gods.

A message just for her.

As blood begins to drip from her earlobes, I do not feel pity. Just tiredness. Although it was a welcome distraction to wrestle with something other than my conscious, I've grown weary of this war.

As I near her, the pointed spikes pull towards her as if she were magnetic. With each step I take the vibrating intensifies. The Trident shakes with mounting energy, forcing me to tighten my grip.

I close my eyes and lurch the weapon towards her. "Goodbye, Kestrel."

A stormy display of waves and lightning erupts from the points. The velocity and ferociousness of the energy being channelled through the instrument threatens to shatter me. I toe the sand and hold my ground as colossal power runs through my hands.

Within a few seconds, the blast dissipates. The Trident eases its pulsing, returning to an inmate solid object. Once I regain control over my trembling hands and chattering jaw, I bravely open to eyes to find the gods have taken her.

Nothing but charred sand and rising steam lies before me.

She's gone. Vanished. Exiled.

For the first time in what feels like forever, I sink to my knees and listen to the silence in my head.

The light crunch of footsteps encroaching from behind causes me to glance over my shoulder. Who knew he could step so quietly?

"That must not have been easy for you."

The gentleness in Kellan's voice tugs at my core. He lowers himself to sit beside me, resting his shield before us.

I shrug not knowing what to say. It was not a matter of ease or struggle, or whether I got satisfaction from the deed or not. Much like when I defeated the Soleil fleet, I tell myself I simply did what had to be done.

I simply did what had to be done. I simply-

"Wren?" he says, not much louder than a whisper.

I pause my inner panicking, twisting to see his good arm, open and inviting. He nods towards his chest and waits for me to lean into him.

I inch towards him before freezing, "Wait, where's Callum?"

Kellan jerks his chin down the bay, "Your people are taking care of him."

I follow his gaze to see big-bellied Rhea and another young siren have shed their tail-skirts and have braved their legged form to aid Callum. He's sitting upright against a pier pole, hanging his head in his hands. I'm sure he'll have a gigantic headache, but he's alive, that's all I care about.

Sighing, I sag into Kellan's chest. He wraps his arm around me, the good arm, I doubt he can even bend the other.

"I'm sorry you got hurt because of me," I mutter, not able to look at him, "Again."

"Ah, it's a mere scratch," he mumbles, retracting it behind his back so I cannot see it, "It takes a lot more to kill me. Are you injured?"

I roll my shoulders, but I shake my head not wanting to complain, after all this whole ordeal feels like my fault, "I'm...I'll recover."

Kellan takes one look at my spine and throws me an arch brow. Feathers stick to my skin due to dried blood, and a mixture of ichor and sand cake every inch of my back.

He softly thumbs the curvature of my wings, "My little Wren."

"I'm not little," I rebut, my wings fluttering in frustration and threaten to unfurl.

Hmm. I'll have to ask advice from the harpies about control my new additions.

"Oh," he chuckles, "I like you when you're angry."

"Wings, or no wings I have always been angry."

"Perhaps, I've always liked you then," he says soberly and lightly kisses my forehead.

I sit with him holding me for a few minutes, knowing when the time comes to stand, I will be stepping into a different life. Time moves fast in the mortal world, but a moment spent with Kellan is never a wasted one.

We sit for a few minutes before I sigh once more and find my feet. The magical realm has waited long enough for a fair ruler, I won't keep them waiting any longer.

Kellan rises beside me, and carefully hands me the Trident before lifting his Shield. He casts a gaze as the syrens who have gathered in the bay, and the harpies flying overhead. They're waiting to bring me home.

Callum and Rhea stagger their way up the bay towards us. Granted, Rhea wobbles due to never using her legs on land before and has the added weight of a pregnancy belly, whereas Callum limp is wound-induced, but it's a heart-warming sight to see them linked arm in arm and aiding each other.

"You must mend your Kingdom," I say after a beat, nodding towards his broken brother and damaged town, "And I must heal my Queendom."

Gazing into the distance, I move away. Syren's do not feel cold but stepping further from him causes my skin to become peppered with goosebumps. I cross my arms to prevent me from reaching out to him. My stiffening shoulders pull my wings forward. They gently caress my arms, wrapping around to hug me.

He nods, and straightens his stature, "Does this make us enemies?"

"I don't think we were ever enemies," I offer with a weak smile, fighting away tears as I leave the brothers to their reunion.

I walk a few strides alone before Rhea reaches out her hand. I'm not sure if the support is for her benefit or mine, but together we take

Together Rhea and I take baby steps towards the waves. Without glancing back, we swim to the rest of the syrens. Hippocampi swim before us and harpies overhead as I lead my people back to Seven Spikes and the Water World. For the first time ever, I make my way *home*.

TWENTY-FOUR

One Month Later.

Even though I've spent nearly every day in the Temple since stepping foot on the Seven Spike mainland, the sheer size of pantheon before me still takes me by surprise.

It stuns me almost as much as the number of people piling into it. As the last few stragglers make their way through the tall stone columns lining the entrance, Rhea twists me around so I only look at her.

"Hey, try not to focus on the crowds," she suggests, straightening out the front of my dress. She sweeps back my loose hair with a look of annoyance but thankfully she doesn't badger me to braid it again. Once I told her I wanted Dove to be the last person who ever plaited it, she nodded with understanding and begrudgingly let me wear my hair down.

"I don't think there's a syren left in the sea or a harpy in the trees," I say, trying to joke but the nervousness in my voice is overwhelming.

"Is hardly seems like a bad thing to bring everyone down to earth?" Rhea asks with a wide grin.

A shadow descends onto our faces as Aengus comes to a halt beside us. Even among his fellow centaurs, he stands a solid foot and a half over them. His imposing stature, knowledge of leadership and good reputation are what secured his place as my right-hand-man of the land, whereas Rhea is what I like to call my left-hand-woman of the seas. With them guiding me on either side, it was unlikely I'll wander off the straight and narrow path.

"Wings out, and chin up," Aengus says, before bowing slightly at the hips. He turns on his hooves and walks his way towards the heavy oak doors with his tail swishing behind him

"All rise." His stern bellow echoes through the aisles and is followed by the immense rustling of fabric and shuffling of feet. Gods above, how many people were in there?

Rhea gives my hands one last squeeze, before following him inside. I take a step after her, but she raises a graceful palm upwards, pausing me. Once she is sure I won't coward behind her like a child, she waddles her way inside, and for the first time all day, I'm alone.

I count to five, roll my shoulders four times, take three deep breathes, glance at my two feet and then take one step forward.

Keeping my chin high as instructed means I thankfully avoid looking at the beaming faces on either side of the aisle. Once I am at the top of the Temple, I remain facing forward.

Aengus had insisted I spend hours each day reading ritual preparation passages and practising my chants. Whereas Rhea seemed confident with her advice that I should just say the prayer response anytime I'm unsure what's happening, and I *should* be okay.

Realising the goblin priest overseeing the ceremony is awaiting a reaction from me, I opt to try Rhea's technique.

"*Pánta,*" I offer quietly, bow my head in prayer and chastise myself for not paying attention.

Muddling my way through the opening part of the ceremony, I manage to stave off embarrassment long enough to reach the anointment stage.

First up is Rhea, clutching a slender, cone-shaped seashell. She lifts the shell high for the crowd to see before carefully pouring the contains into the bronze cauldron before us.

"I represent the finned. Syren. Mermen. Mermaid."

She steps aside, letting Aengus take her place.

He singlehandedly raises a curved horn into the air, "I represent the hooved. Centaurs. Minotaur. Satyr."

He adds his offering to the pot, although not as delicately as Rhea. The priest frowns a little as splatters land on the floor.

Finally comes Sage. A friendly a shy young woman who I'd initially mistaken for a wingless harpy, then I assumed she was a nymph that could leave the water; turns out she's a mix of both. The woodland fairy ducks beneath Aengus' elbow, and flashes me a blushing smile.

"I represent the fae. Dryad. Harpy. Nymph," she says, presenting a single foxglove flower. Each magenta trumpet holding a different offering. She rises onto tiptoe and pours it into the cauldron concoction. All three bow before me, then return to their pew.

The priest lightly plucks a feather from the base of my wing and uses it to stir the ichor, blood, somewhat gross mixture.

He calls on Athena to offer me her eternal wisdom, before placing a drop of ichor against my lips and thanking the goddess Veritas for a syren's truthfulness. He glides his hands downward, blessing the soft skin of my sides where my gills emerge. Drawing his hands together, they meet in the centre of my heart where he smears the ancient symbol for courage above my heart.

The irony of me instantly growing tense and releasing a shaky breath isn't lost on the priest nor I. Glancing at the symbol smeared on my chest, I silently pray it grants me the bravery it depicts.

"Are you sure you want to alter the ritual?" the goblin askes discreetly.

I give him a sole nod and repeat the orders Aengus gave me in my mind to at least appear confident.

Wings out, chin up. Wings out, chin up.

Following my wishes, the priest skips the next part of the ritual. He slides his hands over my stomach saying nothing and goes straight to anointing the soles of my feet.

My citizens do not erupt in a swarming mob of hatred and confusion like I've been dreaming about all week. They remain as quiet and respectful as always, but there is a shift in the air and a subtle whisper amongst the crowd.

Thankfully the slight wobble in my legs looks just looks like a balance issue instead of my crippling nervousness.

With the ritual complete, I finally turn to face my people and that's when I see him.

Kellan.

Donning his golden ceremonial attire and bronze crown atop his fair hair, he catches every drop of light pouring through the stained glass, but truth be told it's his wide, wolfish grin I notice most.

I've never seen anyone look so proud of me.

To his left sit Fletcher and Callum, with Aveen, Arthur and two other sailors filling the rest of the pew.

I instantly want to make my way towards them, but I'm quickly ushered into a kneeling stance once more by the priest. Even though I cannot see Kellan from my lowered stance, just knowing he's there eases my nerves.

With his hands being of smaller stature, the coral crown looks huge within the goblins hold. The hefty headpiece is placed upon my head, and although I worried about it being too heavy, or slipping off, it's a perfect fit.

Poseidon's Trident is placed in my right hand.

"A ruler to reign over the magic realm and guide the creatures of the soil, sky and sea, I present you to your people. Arise Queen Wren of the Water World, and Seven Spikes."

This time I do not wobble as I stand. As I rise, so too do my people. The crowd erupts.

The Temple becomes alive with chattering, as guest step outside to allow the banquet to be set up. I try to spot Kellan and the rest of the Lunar crew, but they must have already filed out with the crowd.

Once my crown and Trident are carefully removed for safekeeping, I try to make my way down the central aisle, but hands touch me from every angle.

Trying not to seem ungrateful, I grin and bear the discomfort that strangers clutching at me brings and accept their blessings with a humble smile.

"Let the Queen through," Aengus bellows whilst lifting a pew onto his shoulder.

Wordlessly the crowd parts, bowing as they step out of the way. I fight the urge to bow back as I know Aengus would chastise me.

Once outside, my eyes immediately begin scanning the hordes of creatures and citizens for them, but they're nowhere to be seen. I used to be able to spot Kellan a head's height above everyone else, but with my citizens' height varying wildly, there's no such luck here.

A blow from behind threatens to knock me off my feet. I spin to find the knee-high projectile is none other than Aveen.

"Wren, you have wings now!" she exclaims, shaking her little head in disbelief. Intricate braids are twisted around her golden tiara to help keep it atop the energetic princess's head.

"Calm, *mikros.*" A deep voice rumbles from behind.

214

Aveen spins me around with such speed I almost fall into Kellan. He catches my elbow instantly and steadies me wordlessly.

"Congratulations, your Majesty," Fletcher offers, as he and Callum appear behind Kellan. When I physically shudder at the word, they all laugh.

"You don't ever get used to it," Kellan mutters quietly, thumbing the small of my back where no-one else can see.

"Where should he place these?" Callum asks, gesturing towards the armful of gifts burdening Arthur.

With a judging eye, Callum searches the nearby buildings and horizons, yet I know he will not find what he's looking for.

"There is no palace or castle building here. The main Queendom is beneath us," I explain, trying not to laugh as Aveen stomps her feet as if to activate a magical portal, "The land creatures are itching to build me a fortress, but I prefer using the Temple for any official work. It's a stark reminder I work here to *serve* the gods agenda, not my own."

A collective nod makes its way through the group. We've all witnessed the unfortunate catastrophe of a selfish Queen growing above her post.

"Do you spend much time in the Water World?" Fletcher asks, staring at the seas surrounding the isle. I don't have the heart to tell him he's facing the completely wrong direction.

"No, thankfully Rhea oversees the general running of everything past the Clam Gates. And when I am below the waves, I have Aengus to keep a *tight rein* on things up here," I add, loud enough for the nearby centaur to hear me.

As usual, he rolls his eyes at my horse-pun but sets down the pew he's carrying and introduces himself to the group. Everyone is somewhat enamoured with him, although Aveen seems a little more so and Kellan a little less.

"Can I trot him around the town?" Aveen squeals.

"No," Kellan and Aengus say in harmony.

When Aveens lower lip wobbles, Aengus knits his eyebrows, confused by the small, emotional child.

"Well, I must finish preparing the Temple for the banquet, but I'm sure..." Aengus' voice trails off as he scans the crowd for a victim, "I'm sure Tarlock would be honoured to show the Princess around."

Upon hearing his name, the centaur colt drops the pew in his arms and trots over with an eager face. He bows in a clumsy fashion, before carefully boosting Aveen onto his dappled grey back.

With outstretched arms, Kellan offers to take the gifts from Arthur and instead gives him and the other sailors a wordless nod to follow his sister.

"I'll go too," Callum announces flatly, wandering after them.

Fletcher waits until his husband is out of earshot to say, "He doesn't mean to question the fidelity of your citizens, but coronations but him on edge."

I nod understandably, and he tags along with the Aveen parade leaving Kellan and me alone.

"I best place these somewhere safe before the feast begins," Kellan says quietly, his eyes giving me a knowing look, "Do you have somewhere away from the crowds? Somewhere more secluded?"

"Follow me," I smirk.

TWENTY-FIVE

Stepping inside my door, I discreetly kick a pile of clothes under my bed. If my messy home wasn't evidence enough that I rarely entertain guest, Kellan slamming face-first into the invisible wall at the threshold ought to do it.

"Sorry!" I yelp, picking up the parcels he dropped, "I forgot the doorway is enchanted. The fae cast a spell it so only people invited in may enter. It was the only way Aengus would let me stay without constant guards."

Even after I invite him in, he moves warily through the hidden forcefield of magic, rubbing his jaw from the impact, "I reluctantly find myself agreeing with him. It's hardly the castle you deserve."

"I don't want a castle, I want a home," I shrug.

My humble home is small.

Technically, it's only one room and not even a cottage anymore since I replaced the bathroom door with a heavy curtain I have drawn back most of the time. Being able to see every corner gives my mind a sense of ease before I sleep.

Eating my meals with my people and having no cooking skills, meant I had little need for a kitchen. Instead, I gave away every pot, pan and piece of cutlery to the cooking fae, except for the lone mug on my windowsill in which I grow a daffodil.

As I clear a section of my table for Kellan to place the gifts, I mutter under my breath, "I'm assuming you didn't get my messenger shell that specifically stated no gifts?"

He shrugs off his ceremonial jacket and folds it across the table. Slipping his hand into the pocket, he pulls out a creamy coloured clamshell, "This shell?"

Yep. That shell. The shell I sang my invitation and gave strict '*no gifts*' orders into. More importantly, the shell in which I stupidly told him how much I needed him. How I feared the binding oath had changed me irrevocably as I felt a part of me was still being drawn back to him. How I had grown to realise the idea of '*home*' might be a feeling more so than a location.

Feeling flustered, I know my cheek have flushed lilac, "Well if you received my damn shell, why did you ignore my request? You also disregarded the time I told you to arrive! Did you even listen to a single word I said?"

With an arched eyebrow, he closes the space between us with a single stride. He nestles the shell onto of his jacket, carefully, as if it were the most precious object he possessed, "I listened to *every* word you said, but the ending was my favourite. You know, I snuck off to the shoreline in the depth of night a few nights ago and tried to sing into a shell? I spend half the night in the sea, snapping shells in half trying to capture the message quickly. The only bloody shell I did manage to shut properly sunk to the bottom of the sea when I skimmed the damn thing. I wanted you to inform you I'd be bringing gifts regardless of what you said, and also that I'd be coming to your coronation, not just the feast afterwards. Did you really think I wouldn't see you be crowned because the *'the ritual is bizarre and bloody'*?"

I roll my eye at his mocking of me, but motion to the symbols and thumb marks of dried blood that dot my body, "It is! Quite literally bloody. I thought you would find the ceremony too strange and hard to follow."

He shakes his head, "It was certainly enchanting, but not strange. The only part I didn't understand is why the crowd gasped when that troll anointed your feet?"

Shit.

Of course, he would notice that.

The real reason I didn't want him to attend my ritual bubbles up. Heavens knows I'm good at skirting around the truth, but if I want my reign to be an honest one, I must start off on a good note.

"My people weren't gasping at the anointing of my soles. They were surprised at the step before it that was skipped," I explain, pulling out of his hold, "I...I asked the priest not to pray for my fertility or bless my womb."

He nods, pulling me back in tight as if he cannot bear to have distance between us. He runs a tender hand through my hair in a soothing, stroking action.

His silence is deafening.

"Are you not going to ask me why?" I press.

A coy smile pulls at the corner of his lips, "Interrogation was the old way we used to communicate. We have new and improved ways."

He cranes his neck downwards, pressing his warm, velvety lips against mine. My mouth falls open to accepting him entirely without any resistance. Gods above, his mouth is somehow more soft and supple than I remembered. On the rare night I said to Hel with it and allowed myself to fall asleep imagining this moment, I still didn't do it justice.

Focus, Wren, focus.

It takes me a Cyclops amount of self-restraint to raise a hand to pause him.

"I don't want children," I blurt out.

He reels his head back a few inches and looks as if he's going to start a lecture, so I continue before he gets the chance to.

"I know that's what is expected of syrens, especially of Queens, but I can't. I have an entire Queendom to restructure. I plan on being the last monarch because I'm implementing a voting system, where each creature faction would have its own ruler. I want to ensure a Kestrel-like tyranny never happens again. So see, I won't even need an heir. Not that I would ever have a child for that reason, I'm not my mother. But, I just wanted you to know.... I'm not trying to ramble, it's just-

"Wren," he says sternly, "Stop being ridiculous."

My breath catches in my throat at his harshness. Does he think me ridiculous for not wanting children or for telling him in the first place? I used to get an inch in my legs when panic surged inside of me, but now I get a tingle between my shoulder blades as wings remind me I can flea to the skies.

"You do not owe me or anyone an explanation."

He speaks slowly, making sure each word sinks in, "Your citizens and creatures are incredibly lucky to have someone as selfless as you. On the day of your coronation, you're planning to dismantle the throne and give these people power? You couldn't be your mother if you tried."

Selfless? No-one had ever called me that before.

He leans in to kiss me again, but I duck away.

"I mean it, Kellan. After growing up with a mother like mine, I don't ever want to be a mother to someone else. I won't change my mind," I say honestly, surprising myself at how easily the words pass through my lips.

"I'm aware. You're incredibly strong-willed and stubborn when you set your mind to something," he exhales, staring at my lips impatiently, "But how many times must I tell you, together or not at all."

"Well me opting for *not at all,* means that we can't do the *together* part, Kellan. You'll need an heir for the Lunar Lands and Soleil," I try to sound diplomatic.

Business-like and regal. As if we were simply discussing how to attack another isle because if I let my emotion slip in, I will fall apart.

"I don't need an heir. You're not the only one planning on stepping away from the crown. I'm simply keeping the throne warm until Aveen comes of age, and then I'm abdicating," he shrugs.

"What? Why?" I gasp.

"When my father died, I was thrown into this position by the councilmen. I was forced to shake off the grieving orphan title faster than my siblings because someone had to step up to the crown. I became a leader for the people, a father figure to Aveen, and well, it's a steep learning curve and I've fucked up a couple times. I've been King less than a year and I've already stolen a neighbouring isle I was directly told not to," he sighs looking weary with himself.

He runs a hand through his hair and adds, "I'll rule for a decade, figure out all the hard parts and make things easier for my sister. She's far more temperate than I'll ever be. She's already receiving a strict education, and we'll teach her everything she needs to know. She'll have Callum and me for warfare, Fletcher for naval tactics and you for marine life and magic. Aveen is too young to have lost so much, this is the one thing I can give her. She deserves this."

I cannot help but smile and blink away swelling emotions as I'm mentioned in these future plans, "You're a very good brother."

"I'll have to be around for Aveen as Master of the Wars, or an emotional punching bag, or official hair-braider, whatever it is she needs. But we could spend the winter months there and reside here for the summers if you desire?"

"Ah, you wish to make me Persephone," I muse.

"Gods above, I hope you don't think of me as Hades," he rasps, "But yes, I need to have you by my side, or be beside you, so long as we are *together* instead of *not at all*. Because I can never spend another sleepless night skimming and sinking shells, desperately trying to tell you how I missed you to a harrowing degree."

My heart lurches forward, the way it only does around him.

He plants a light kiss against my forehead, and selects a long, narrow box from the pile, "Now, open the present I brought you."

I think about protesting once more, but realistically I don't want to. The box is beautifully wrapped. He gives a single encouraging nod, and I prise open the lid.

With a gasp, I carefully unfold the fabric, recognising the handiwork anywhere. Another delicate dress, crafted by Shelli, except this one is adapted to have openings for my gills and wings. With its deep hue of navy, and shimmering silver highlighting the bodice, it's the perfect representation of Seven Spikes.

I stand up and slip out of my ceremonial robe without warning, letting it land in a puddle fabric on the floor. Kellan takes a sharp inhale, his eyes roaming over every inch of my bare skin. I use his toned shoulder to balance myself as I step into Shelli's beautiful creation. I shimmy it upwards until it hugs my hips. Even before it's closed, I can tell it fits perfectly.

"Allow me," he offers with a hoarse voice. The gown is backless to account for my wings. Six buttons trial from the small of my back to the base of my tailbone.

Even though he's hands are big and calloused, his nimble fingers manage to close them without a problem, although he does take his time. With a single finger, he trails a gentle touch along my spine, between my wings and across the base of my neck.

As I melt into his hold, he wraps a steadying hand around my waist, and whispers into my ear, "I've one more present for you."

He slips his hand into his trousers pocket, grazing against my backside more than necessary, but I don't complain.

"The dress is a gift from a King to a Queen to mark her coronation, but this is a gift just from Kellan to Wren."

Over my shoulder, he hands me a slender, leather pouch with holster strap, and bronze clasp the same shade as his eyes, "Happy Birthday."

Hearing him say that sends cold chill rushing through me. My mind become bombarded with omen flashbacks of the Trident prong through his chest, the Luring Lullaby and everything else that could have been.

Could have been, I remind myself with a steadying deep breath. It's not often one alters Fate, and I certainly could not have done it alone. Needing to make sure this moment it real, that we really did survive everything, I twist to see him.

With a wide grin, he waits with eager eyes for me to open the gift. Shaking off any bad memories, I allow myself to be happy and enjoy this fleeting moment entirely. Times passes by quick in the mortal realm, and I don't want to waste a second worrying about how could have been.

I unbuckle the clasp and carefully withdraw a damascus steel knife. It's a replicate of his, except mine has not been dulled from use.

"It's exquisite," I admit, admiring the elaborate detail, "Absolutely perfect in case anyone tries to kidnap me with a net."

I lurch forward instantly, and lightly push the tip of the blade under his jaw. He swallows hard, but he does not flinch nor blink. Lowering the blade with a scowl, I mutter, "I wish you were even just the *tiniest* bit afraid of me."

"Wren, I'm absolutely terrified of the power you hold over me," he admits, taking the knife from me.

He grips the handle between his teeth, drops onto a bended knee and hoists up the weighted skirt of my dress onto his shoulder. He begins strapping the blade to my inner thigh, "But this weapon isn't intended for me. Some of the creatures here are impervious to your song. There's no harm in being armed just in case anyone gets too close. Take Aengus for example."

Try as he might to sound casual, jealously saturates every word. As he drapes my dress over the holster, I can't help but laugh, "Now you know how I feel about Nessa."

He rises to his feet, "Nessa? Gods no, I prefer women more..."

"More stubborn? More trouble? More gilled or winged?" I muse, making my way towards the door.

As much as I wanted to stay away from the crowds, to stay here with him, I think Rhea would finally go into labour if I was late for my own feast.

"Just *more*," he says firmly, coming to a halt with his frame filling the doorway, "It's hard for me to explain, but you have this depth to you, one filled with torment and nightmares, that's sharply contrasted by the lightness of your laugh. You're the crescendo and the silence all at once. The deepest sea to the highest sky, and everything in between. You're the very spectrum of what it is to be alive, and so much more."

He lightly kisses my forehead before making his way outside. Rolling up his crisp white shirt in the spring sunshine, he offers me his heavily scarred left arm, "Come, introduce me to your wonderfully diverse citizens."

I take his arm without hesitation, "It would be an honour. You know, one of my mermaids spotted an abandoned island about thirty miles east of here. It sounds ripe for the taking...."

We stroll arm in arm towards the feast, plotting our future conquers and planning our lives.

I may have given up immortality but knowing Kellan has led me to believe that one life is more than enough if you cherish every second.

Keep up to date with Naomi Kelly publications, giveaways, and upcoming events by following:

 naomikellywriting

 Naomi Kelly Writing

Head over to Goodreads to find reviews and quotes about Meraki, and feel free to leave your own thoughts too!